"I've ne̶̶̶ ̶̶̶ ̶̶̶ ̶̶̶ ̶̶̶ ̶̶̶ ̶̶̶ ̶̶̶ in the audience before."

"Your family?"

"No." Juliet shook her head. "They're busy, busy... You know how it is?"

"I don't."

"I'm sorry." Gosh, how insensitive when his parents were dead, but he smiled at her sudden anguish.

"I meant, growing up... My parents were always front row, much to my horror at times," he elaborated. "My mother liked to make an entrance, then she'd applaud just for me and blow kisses... Thankfully we went to boarding school in Milan or she'd have been embarrassing me through my teenage years too."

He liked the soft sound of her laughter and how it trailed away, as if she understood they were greatly missed on this day... Then he reminded himself of his role and that his absence would soon be noticed. As if to confirm it, in the distance his name was called.

"I should get back."

"And me."

They made no move to go though.

And, despite promises to himself to behave this day, at the eleventh hour he caved. He wanted her tonight.

Rival Italian Brothers

A spicy new duet from USA TODAY *bestselling author Carol Marinelli!*

The Casadios are *the* most prominent family in Lucca, Italy, with a vineyard and palazzo nestled in the Tuscan hills. It was assumed, when dutiful Savendro and his wild younger brother, Dante, were born, the legacy would be passed down to the two heirs. But secrets and tragedy have led to an unsurpassable rift between the brothers...

Now, after years of pursuing their own billion-dollar successes, the brothers have been reunited by their beloved grandfather. But healing old rifts will take more than coming face-to-face with one another. They'll also need to confront the unimaginable passion they find along the way...

Discover Dante and Susie's story in
Italian's Pregnant Mistress

And indulge in Savendro and Juliet's story,
Italian's Cinderella Temptation

Both available now!

ITALIAN'S CINDERELLA TEMPTATION

CAROL MARINELLI

Harlequin

PRESENTS

ISBN-13: 978-1-335-93976-0

Italian's Cinderella Temptation

Copyright © 2025 by Carol Marinelli

Recycling programs
for this product may
not exist in your area.

Harlequin Enterprises ULC
22 Adelaide St. West, 41st Floor
Toronto, Ontario M5H 4E3, Canada
www.Harlequin.com

Printed in Lithuania

MIX
Paper | Supporting
responsible forestry
FSC® C021394

Carol Marinelli recently filled in a form asking for her job title. Thrilled to be able to put down her answer, she put "writer." Then it asked what Carol did for relaxation and she put down the truth—"writing." The third question asked for her hobbies. Well, not wanting to look obsessed, she crossed her fingers and answered "swimming"—but, given that the chlorine in the pool does terrible things to her highlights, I'm sure you can guess the real answer!

Books by Carol Marinelli

Harlequin Presents

Cinderellas of Convenience

The Greek's Cinderella Deal
Forbidden to the Powerful Greek

Scandalous Sicilian Cinderellas

The Sicilian's Defiant Maid
Innocent Until His Forbidden Touch

Heirs to the Romero Empire

His Innocent for One Spanish Night
Midnight Surrender to the Spaniard
Virgin's Stolen Nights with the Boss

Wed into a Billionaire's World

Bride Under Contract
She Will Be Queen

Rival Italian Brothers

Italian's Pregnant Mistress

Visit the Author Profile page
at Harlequin.com for more titles.

PROLOGUE

THE TROUBLE WITH BROTHERS?

They know.

Before heading into the meeting, Sevandro Casadio slid open the private drawer of his desk to collect his wallet and caught sight of a wedding band.

It still startled him—as if a foreign object had been placed in his drawer...something that didn't belong to him. Here in Dubai, aged twenty-three, it still didn't feel real that back home in Lucca he had a wife.

He'd never worn the ring—on his wedding day his hand, thanks to a fight with his brother, had been too swollen. But Sheikh Mahir had made a comment, pointing out that the wedding had been three months ago and surely his hand was better now.

Sev had got the implication. Sheikh Mahir was very much a family man, and his relief had been evident when, a few short weeks after commencing work in Dubai, Sev had told him that he was marrying a girl from home.

'That is excellent.' He had smiled at Sev, the young gun who was determined to make waves in the hotel industry. 'A stable home life is good for business.'

Sev had attended the same prestigious Milan school as the Sheikh's son, Adal. They hadn't particularly been friends—Sev was guarded and did not make friends easily. Still, one year he'd invited Adal to the summer festival in Lucca. In turn, Sev had been invited to spend time in Dubai.

More recently he'd approached Sheikh Mahir, telling him about a hotel in Tuscany that was about to go under and explaining his well-thought-out plan, but Mahir had been uninterested.

'I have enough going on here…'

'I recall you saying you were looking for investment opportunities in Italy.'

'That was when Adal was considering living there. I wanted a project for him.'

'This could be one,' Sev had persisted, knowing very well Adal wouldn't lift a finger, but sensing an in for himself. 'Adal and I get on.'

Barely… But he would take the idle Adal off his father's hands for the duration if that was what it took.

Sev wanted capital and, as he'd told Sheikh Mahir, 'The owners need a quick sale—it's too good to pass up.'

'If it's such a good opportunity, why did your grandfather say no?'

'I haven't discussed it with him,' Sev had admitted. 'I'd prefer to keep family and business separate.'

'An impossible ask.' Sheikh Mahir had sighed heavily. 'Everything we do is for family.' He'd paused then, and taken a long, pondering look at Sev. 'What if I told you I had a project here? Well, it's more Adal's venture…'

It had taken him a moment to register that Mahir was offering him opportunities in both Italy and in Dubai, and Sevandro had embraced both. He'd flown back to

Lucca to celebrate…perhaps celebrated a little too reck-lessly one night…

Sheikh Mahir had been correct.

The moment Sev had found out he was to be a father his priorities had changed. While work had always taken pre-cedence there had always been plenty of time to indulge in his playboy ways. No more. He would work not just to fulfil his own ambitions but for Rosa, and the baby they had made, in a heady, brief encounter.

Everything he did now was for family.

There had been a brief honeymoon, then back to work in Dubai. Rosa did not understand why he didn't remain in Lucca—after all the Casadio Winery was as good his.

She didn't understand that he might want to make his own way.

And he didn't understand the delay in announcing her pregnancy.

'People will talk,' Rosa said. 'Let's wait a few more weeks.'

But then she'd called him in Dubai and told him she was bleeding. He'd flown home immediately—but to the news that their baby was gone…

He'd grieved alone.

Rosa refused to discuss things. Her parents, with whom she was staying, stonewalled him too, calling him insen-sitive.

'It was my baby too,' he'd pointed out, and then called over their shoulders so that Rosa could hear, 'We have an appointment with Dr Romero.'

He'd made several on his many trips home since the loss, but there had always been a reason she couldn't attend.

His family, unaware of the baby's existence, hadn't noticed that Sev, always solemn and serious, was even more so on these trips. His brother Dante might have picked up on it, might have heard he was staying at a hotel, but they were no longer speaking—and anyway, Dante was back in Milan…

In Dubai the frenetic pace continued, with deadlines to be met and meetings to attend, but for now, with his marriage well into injury time, they could wait.

He didn't just want answers—he needed them.

Certainly he wasn't going to put on a wedding band just to appease Sheikh Mahir. Placing it back in the drawer, he looked out at the glittering view of the Persian Gulf.

He took up his phone and was about to call Dr Romero's office to make an appointment to speak with the family doctor and find out what the hell had gone on, when Dante's name flashed across the screen.

At first he thought his brother must be calling to apologise for what he had said about Rosa. Dante's words had been the reason for the groom's swollen hand on his wedding day, and the best man's cut and blackened eyes. Unsure what to say to his brother, he let the call go.

But had Dante been right in his assessment of Rosa? Had there been a baby at all?

Dante called again and this time Sev he answered.

'Sev.'

The moment he heard the strain in his brother's voice, and then a sharp intake of breath, Sev knew this was about more than their fight.

Brothers know.

'I have bad news…' Dante started.

But his words were followed by the ache of a long pause

and Sev's back stiffened, his jaw clenched as he braced himself for whatever was to come.

'The helicopter...' Dante said, referring to the family helicopter that buzzed over the hills regularly. 'It went down just after take-off. The rescuers are on their way.'

'Who?' Sev tried to ask, only no sound came out. 'Who?' he said, this time abruptly, knowing it would likely be their parents, for they used it frequently.

Sadly, he was right. 'They were on their way to Milan to see me.' Dante's voice was strained as he said what he must. 'Sev, Rosa was also on board.'

His reaction was silence, and yet there was a huge roar in his head—so much so that he swung on his chair and looked out of the window, almost expecting to see a fighter jet had gone up. But no, the sky was Dubai-blue and the ocean was glittering and azure as it had been a mere moment ago...

There were no survivors.

Both brothers were pallbearers.

Together, but apart.

Sev helped carry their father's coffin into Lucca's magnificent cathedral. Dante walked behind, helping to carry their mother.

They took their places in the front pew, either side of their grandfather, holding up the devastated Gio. At the cemetery they greeted the mourners, then stood side by side as their parents were buried together.

The wake was held at their property, a huge palazzo on sprawling grounds, set on Lucca's ancient medieval walls. It was an elegant affair, with people speaking in low funeral voices—

'Che tristeza!'

'How sad!'

'Such a vibrant couple...'

'They were so happy...'

'It's so hard to believe just three months ago they were celebrating Sevandro and Rosa's wedding...'

Their voices would trail off for a moment. Then...

'How is he doing?'

No one knew.

Least of all Sev.

Sev had never been one to reveal his feelings, and wasn't about to start on this day.

He could hear the comments, though.

'Have you seen Dante's scar?'

'Hopefully this will reunite the brothers—they need each other now.'

'Twenty-three is far too young to be a widower...'

As the last mourners left, Sev checked in on Gio, who lay pale and fragile on a vast bed, still in his funeral suit.

'I never thought I'd say this,' Gio sobbed as Sevandro undressed him, 'I am glad your *nonna* is dead.' He'd mourned her for as long as Sev could remember. 'This would have been too much for her.'

'Try and rest, Gio,' Sev told him, dimming the sidelight. 'Dante's fetching your tablets and then you need to sleep.'

'Yes...' Gio lay back, closing his eyes on the day he'd buried his son and his daughter-in-law, but then he must have realised there was more grief to come, for he suddenly rallied, reaching for Sev's arm and grabbing the sleeve of his black suit. 'We'll be there for you tomorrow.'

'I know that,' Sev said, looking at the thin pale fingers

clutching his arm, not turning his head as Dante came in with Gio's medicine.

'Dante?' Gio said, even deep in mourning attempting to heal the brothers' rift. 'I think you should help carry Rosa's coffin tomorrow—'

'No need,' Sev interrupted. 'It's all taken care of.'

He stood and left Dante to say goodnight to their grandfather and walked down the long corridor, taking the stairs up to the floor that had once been his and Dante's. Stepping into his old bedroom, he flicked open his case and started to pack, only briefly glancing up as Dante came to the door. The scar that ran through his eyebrow was an angry pink. Garish and vivid. But then so too were the memories of their fight on the eve of his and Rosa's wedding.

'You're packing?'

Sevandro said nothing.

'Are you going to stay with Rosa's parents?'

Sevandro made a slight hissing noise, one that said, *When hell freezes over*—or at least it did to the brother who had once known him so well.

'So where?'

Sev gritted his teeth and snapped the case closed.

'Don't stay at a hotel tonight…'

Sev had been staying at hotels a lot since his marriage, but he wasn't about to discuss that with Dante now and, picking up his case, he left.

'Sevandro.' His brother bounded down the stairs behind him, then beat him to the vast doors. 'Please…' He attempted to halt him. 'What I said on the eve of your wedding—'

'Not now,' Sev cut in. No, he didn't want to hear it on the eve of Rosa's funeral. 'Just—'

He could not complete his sentence. Since the news had hit—since the roar like a fighter jet had faded—he'd been numb. Completely numb and unable to place a label on a single feeling. He didn't know if it was grief, or anger, or even guilt because he'd never loved his wife. It was as if a fog had descended and wrapped around him, seeping into his veins, sedating all emotion. And that was how he'd got on the plane home. That was how he'd dealt with his family, as well as Rosa's, and yet now the fog seemed to lift for a moment, a brief surge of something hitting him—and it was something he could finally label.

Protectiveness.

A surge of protection towards Rosa.

Tomorrow he would lay his young wife to rest in the ground. However bad the private hell of their marriage had been, tomorrow he would do the right thing by her. He looked at his brother and thought of all Dante had once said about Rosa and knew there would be no reconciliation tonight.

'We'll keep things polite for the sake of Gio, but don't even think about carrying her coffin tomorrow,' Sev warned him. 'Or I'll put a matching scar over the other eye.'

Rosa's service was held in the church they had been married in. Out of town, it was nestled in the foothills of Lucca, close to both families' wineries. Sev, along with Rosa's father and her cousins, carried the coffin. Watching her being lowered into the ground all he could hear was their final row, when once again she'd refused to see a doctor or answer any of the many questions he had.

'Please don't leave me, Sevandro,' she'd sobbed. *'What will people think?'*

Her wake was held at the smaller De Santis Winery, and Sev felt a hypocrite as he accepted the handshakes and condolences. Rosa's parents, who had known he was on the edge of ending the marriage, seemed to have forgotten all about that—they sobbed and spoke of the happy couple and how in love they had been.

It was hardly the place to correct them.

Stepping outside, he walked away from the rather dilapidated cellar door, where the mourners were gathered, and found a secluded spot. But there was no solace there. The wreckage of the helicopter was still in the hills ahead of him.

Dante came and joined him, leaning on a fence. 'How are you holding up?'

Sev didn't answer, because he didn't know himself.

'It's pretty grim in there.'

'Well, what did you expect?' Sev responded, not turning his head, just staring at the wreckage. But then he had a question for his brother. 'Why were they going to Milan?'

'Rosa was attending Fashion Week.'

'I know that.' He'd found out that Rosa had asked his mother to secure her an invitation—clearly, she had recovered quickly from their final row. 'But our parents weren't attending—they were going to have lunch with you. Why?'

'To talk about us,' Dante admitted. 'You and I. They wanted to know why we'd fallen out.' He could feel his brother's eyes on him. 'Sev, I should never have said what I did that night. I don't know if studying law has made me cynical, but at the time I really thought Rosa might be just *saying* she was pregnant.'

Rosa had been saying exactly that.

'Sev,' Dante continued with urgency. 'I was worried

she might be trying to trap you into marriage. Clearly, I was wrong.'

Sev did think of correcting Dante—telling him that very possibly he'd been right. Dr Romero had been there at the funeral, and Sev had even thought of making another appointment to see him, getting the answers to the questions he'd been coming around to asking before the news of the accident had come in.

For what purpose, though?

While he might have married Rosa out of duty, it didn't end just because she'd died... There was the scent of soil in his nostrils, the memory of her last words—how she'd cared what others might think.

So he did not reveal to his brother the hell his marriage had been. Instead he pushed up from the wall he had been leaning on to head back to the wake and accept the handshakes and condolences and honour other people's memory of Rosa.

'Leave it,' he said to his brother.

'Sev...'

'Let her rest.'

It was all he could do for Rosa now.

CHAPTER ONE

Almost ten years later...

'THIS WAY...'

From beneath the hood of her coat, Juliet Adams resisted rolling her eyes as Louanna walked ahead of the small group—she was clearly in good spirits.

It was damp and misty, and Juliet was worried.

There were grey clouds over the Tuscan hills and they seemed headed their way.

Beneath the hood her long red hair was worn down, but clipped back from her face, there were pearls in her ears and the black halter neck dress she wore was more suited to a cocktail party than the middle of the day...

It wasn't her hair or her attire that concerned Juliet, though. It was the instruments they carried. 'Louanna we can't play outside.'

'But it's Valentine's Day in Lucca,' Louanna insisted, carrying her cello case with practised ease. 'Lots of love and music to be made.'

There were four of them. Juliet was English, the others Italian, and they all attended the music school here in Lucca and had formed a string quartet—though offers for work weren't exactly pouring in. Lucca was full to the brim with talented and emerging musicians, and their little ensemble was struggling to get bookings.

Juliet was in her final year and hoping to turn professional soon—though she had exams to focus on and, given her work commitments at the ice-cream store and a local bar, she was behind on practice.

Behind on everything…

Louanna, the cellist and their self-proclaimed manager, had decided to capitalise on this romantic day and persuaded them to perform for free on Lucca's famous ancient walls.

'It's threatening rain.' Ricco glanced up at the ominous sky. 'Look, we can't play. Why don't we head to the square…set up somewhere sheltered?' He nudged Juliet. 'For Valentine's Day they're holding speed-dating there. You could give it a go.'

'Sorry?'

'Speed-dating—it's great fun.'

'In the square?' she checked. 'You mean, in front of everyone?'

'Maybe try it. That is how Gabriele and I met…'

Juliet could honestly not imagine anything more horrific—she was shy at the best of times, but to have an audience watching you blush and bluster your way through first introductions…!

'It's perfect,' Ricco insisted.

He was always trying to matchmake, and lately Juliet seemed to be his project. She found she could talk a little with him—perhaps because he only liked men.

'You say you don't have time to meet anyone…' he went on. 'There will be ten, maybe twelve guys on each table.

It's short—a timed session. If you don't get on with some-one it will drag, but if you click...'

'Oh, please.' Juliet had never *clicked* with anyone. 'What would I say?'

'They'll know you're English, they'll see you're gor-geous. Say you're studying music and hope to be a profes-sional musician,' he turned. 'What else?'

'There isn't much else.' It was the truth—she lived and breathed music and worked to support it. 'I could say I'm hoping to get my residency here...'

'Too much, too soon,' Ricco said. 'Keep it light.' He thought for a moment. 'Okay, what's your ideal first date?'

'A nice restaurant?'

'You're as broke as me.'

'A picnic, then. Flowers? I don't know...'

'Just be yourself. But don't go on about your exes...'

'I'm not doing it,' Juliet said, rather than tell him that there weren't any exes.

Well, hardly.

She'd never got past the getting-to-know-you part—or rather, when her date got to know that she'd never seriously dated, let alone slept with anyone, any fledgling romance came to an abrupt end.

As if being twenty-five and a virgin, and seriously sin-gle, meant she must have issues...

'Give it a go,' Ricco pushed, but she shook her head.

'I'll think about it once my exams are out of the way...'

'What is there to think about?

She was saved from answering by a welcome drizzle of rain, and Dario spoke up. 'I'm not playing outside in this.'

'Okay.' Louanna turned around and put up a hand to halt both their protests and their steps. 'We're not playing on the walls—we have a booking...' She pointed to a bench. 'Perhaps take a seat?'

Louanna was a little bossy—albeit effectively so, because they all did as they were told as Louanna stood leaning against the stone wall.

'You've all rehearsed the piece I suggested?' Louanna checked, nodding to Juliet because, given they shared a flat, she would have heard that she had. Ricco and Dario said they'd practised too. 'That's good, because we have a wedding booking.'

'When?' Dario asked.

'Right now!' Louanna said. 'Six hours' paid work and hopefully good tips.'

'Why on earth didn't you say?' Juliet sat up. 'I've been panicking about giving up a shift!'

'I know, but this is a top-secret event. It's Gio Casadio's wedding,' Louanna said, as if that name alone explained everything.

Actually, it did.

'The owner of the Casadio Winery?'

'Yes—amongst many other things.' Louanna nodded. 'Serious wealth. This is the break we've been hoping for.'

'But...' Juliet shook her head at the impossibility of them playing at such an elite function. And it had to be elite— the wine they produced was so well-renowned that even in England she'd heard of it. Not that she'd ever tried it.

Then she swallowed. Actually, she had...

Susie—her and Louanna's flatmate—had brought some home the other week, along with some other fabulous treats, and invited them to help themselves...

Juliet loathed rumours, but she'd have to be living under a rock not to know that Susie and the very out-of-town

Dante Casadio had supposedly had a fling when he'd briefly returned.

'This is huge for us,' Louanna said. 'I nearly died when the event planner called. She asked for our demo tapes before committing and insisted I keep it to myself.'

'I'd have told everyone,' Ricco freely admitted. 'Are you for real, Louanna? Gio is getting married? He must be eighty?'

'The bride isn't much younger!' Louanna had saved the best to last. 'It's Mimi!'

Ricco was so excited to hear Mimi's name that he jumped off the bench and covered his mouth, moaning with excitement.

'Mimi?' Juliet gulped. She knew that name—and not just because the woman was helping Susie with her Italian. 'The famous opera singer?'

'That's the one,' Louanna smiled.

Mimi was incredible.

As soon as she'd heard who it was helping her friend learn Italian, Juliet had fallen into an opera-shaped rabbit hole and started listening to her—studying her, really. Mimi, if she so chose, could stand right where they were now, on the walls, and her voice would reach the beautiful Tuscan hilltops in the distance.

'Why us?' Juliet asked, feeling sick with nerves. 'She could have anyone.'

'They wanted no fuss…just a small family meal after the service…but Gio has decided to surprise her. Mimi has no idea that there's to be live music. Pearla's is catering…'

'Pearla's?' Juliet frowned, glancing along the walls towards the very exclusive restaurant where Susie worked. *Oh, goodness…* 'Is the reception being held at the restaurant?'

'No, no.' Louanna said. 'It's all being held at Gio's home—the planner is there setting up now. Pearla's are tearing their hair out at the short notice—Valentine's is their busiest day. But of course they're not going to say no to Gio. And musically everyone was already booked.'

'Are both Sevandro and Dante going to be there?' Dario asked. Then he added for Juliet's benefit. 'They're Gio's grandsons.'

'Yes, as well as Mimi's sister. It's really small, just a party of five, so there's no room for error...' Louanna warned. They all knew that a bigger audience was in many ways easier. 'Today could lead to much bigger things, so we have to get everything right. There're a few details to run through. Juliet, you especially need to hear this—the guys will know most of it already...'

Juliet nodded. Performing at a wedding wasn't just a matter of plonking down and playing, especially in such an intimate setting as someone's home, so she listened carefully.

'It's a second marriage for both,' Louanna explained. 'Gio's first wife died years ago, whereas Mimi was widowed more recently. She moved in with Gio apparently to help him in the house—though I think they told people that to keep things above board. Gio's very old school...that's why they want low key.'

Juliet nodded and smiled, about to pick her violin case up. She assumed they'd discuss the music selections on the way to the venue, as they usually did, but Louanna waved her to sit back down.

'Wait, Juliet, this is important. A few years ago—actually, it must be almost ten—there was a dreadful accident.

Over there.' She pointed out to the hills. 'Gio's son, along with his wife, were travelling to Milan in a helicopter...'

'He was Gio's only child,' Ricco added—which told Juliet he must have died. 'No one survived. It came down just after take-off. My mother actually saw it happen.'

'They were a stunning couple,' Louanna elaborated, as she always did. 'Really prominent here, and so glamorous...'

Juliet looked out to the hills, currently all misty and grey, as Louanna spoke on.

'Sevandro's wife, Rosa, also died in the accident. They'd only been married a few months...she was so beautiful, so young, and there were whispers she was pregnant.'

'She wasn't,' Ricco said. 'My mother—'

'Guys,' Juliet cut in. For while it helped to know what had happened, she didn't need intimate details. She asked instead for more pertinent information. 'So what music's on the forbidden list?'

'Plenty...' Louanna gave a dramatic sigh. 'I've gone through it with the event planner...'

They started to walk as they discussed the musical selections. There was a lot to avoid. Not just from the funerals, but also the younger couple's wedding.

'It's a musical minefield!' Louanna said as they came to a set of huge gates.

She took out her phone to call the organiser and make sure the coast was clear. As they waited Juliet peered in. There were magnificent buildings all over Lucca, and she'd walked past this one often, assuming it was an old palace or a stately home, perhaps a government building. Even now, looking at the fountains and beautiful gardens, it was hard to fathom it was actually someone's home.

'Let's go,' Louanna said as a groundsman let them in. 'We have half an hour to set up and hopefully rehearse that piece.'

'Should we warn Juliet about the brothers?' Ricco queried as they entered the grounds and walked towards the grand residence. But then he told her anyway. 'There was a big fall-out—'

'I don't need to know.' Juliet felt she'd already had enough of a window into their world.

But Louanna carried on regardless. 'They're rarely together, Sevandro's based in Dubai—he's some big shot in the hotel industry—and Dante is in Milan. He's…'

'Fine,' Juliet snapped.

She'd already gleaned from Susie that Dante was a divorce attorney. Oh, please let Susie not have been roped into working at this function…

'They had a big fight the night before Sevandro's wedding,' Louanna rattled on. 'You'll see the scar on Dante's face—'

'I get it!' Juliet said.

She simply loathed unnecessary talk about people—and with good reason. Her parents had broken up thanks to careless gossip. Worse, Juliet was the one who'd caused the break-up, having repeated what she'd overheard at school…

'Sevandro's a cold bastard.' Louanna just loved to talk. 'He doesn't even visit Rosa's grave when he's back. In fact, you might see him in the square,' she added sarcastically. 'He certainly enjoys speed-dating…though I don't think there's much *dating* involved.'

'Stop!' Juliet hated confrontation but, blushing horribly, she turned and faced her. Louanna was simply too much at times. 'We've been invited to play at a family wedding and we are taking their money,' Juliet reminded the group. 'I don't think it's appropriate to be talking so nastily about any of them.'

'I'm just telling you what you need to know.'

'No.' Juliet shook her head. 'I don't need to know that!'

'Juliet's right.' Ricco backed her up. 'Let's go in there and share in their celebration and make the best music we can.'

It was, though, rather daunting…

The event planner led them into a vast entrance hall with an impossibly high ceiling and a curved staircase. It was all so grand and formal that it was even harder to think of it as a home.

'The dining room is being decorated now,' they were told. 'I'll let you know when the wedding group start to head back so you can stop tuning. It's to be a complete surprise.'

'We can store our things here,' Louanna told them, taking out a key and opening up a door beneath the stairs. She turned the lights on. 'I brought the stands over last night.'

It was far too large to be called a cupboard—one wall was lined with hooks and there were long benches. Removing her coat, Juliet guessed it had once been a cloakroom, and could picture grand balls and counts' and countesses' coats and capes being hung there.

It was nice to have a safe place to leave extra instruments, and such—somewhere that drinks wouldn't be spilled or have people tripping over them. And it was a treat to have a suitable place to hang their coats and check their appearance before setting up.

In contrast to the austere entrance hall, the dining room was more welcoming. While very grand, the elegant fur-nishings were rich with family photos and mementoes. French windows led onto a tiled portico and beyond a less formal garden, giving it a cosier feel. It was currently being dressed for the wedding, with portraits of both Mimi and Gio being positioned on easels.

As they set up Louanna nudged her. 'There's Susie— she's in her waitressing gear. I wonder if Dante knows she'll be here?'

Then she must have recalled Juliet's rare outburst and abruptly stopped.

'You could have at least warned her about the wedding,' Juliet chided. 'This morning before we left.'

'I didn't know she would be waitressing,' Louanna retorted. 'I thought she was working in the kitchen at Pearla's now. Anyway, I promised not to reveal anything.'

'But surely…?'

'No.' Louanna shook her head. 'The management at Pearla's have kept it from their staff till the last minute. You told me off for gossiping but now question why Susie wasn't told. You can't have it both ways, Juliet.'

Louanna made a good point—but what about loyalty and friendship? Susie was as pale as a ghost, Juliet thought as she gave her friend a wave. She'd been worried about her for a little while. If she *had* had a fling with Dante, it would be dreadful to have to work at a function he was attending.

It was rather a rush to set up, but they tuned their instruments and then rehearsed the piece they'd practised separately before the event planner called for them all to stop.

'They're at the main gates…'

'Quiet, everyone!' someone else called, and the main doors to the dining room were closed to shut them in.

Susie came out of a small butler's pantry carrying a silver tray with glasses of champagne. She was dreadfully pale, as she had often been of late, and Juliet found her eyes drifting down to Susie's stomach. She was relieved that it looked completely flat, telling herself she was imagining things. But she was truly worried for her new friend.

The pause was long, and they all sat quietly, taking one last look around the beautiful room, and then, as footsteps approached, they took their positions, ready to play.

There was chatter and laughter outside, and then the doors opened…

'Oh!' Mimi gasped, as she stepped in, looking so stunned that she lost that gorgeous voice for a moment as their music gloriously welcomed the bride.

She was dressed in emerald silk, her silver curls piled high, and she walked around; her hands clasped, red lips smiling.

'Oh, Gio…' she kept saying, clearly overcome as she went over to the portraits.

And even though Juliet's ears were on the music they played, the piece was so familiar that she allowed her gaze to drift to Susie, her tray proffered as a man came in.

It was Dante. Juliet knew that not just because she'd seen him on television, more because he and Susie were trying too hard to ignore each other as he took a champagne flute from her tray.

Then the other grandson walked in.

About to turn back to her fellow musicians, return her full attention to the music, suddenly Juliet heard the chatter, the laughter, even the sound from her own violin, seem to fade. It was as if she was observing from one of the audio booths at music school. The world seemed to hush even as she played on.

That must be Sevandro.

He wore not a scowl, but a stern expression—as if he were walking into a funeral rather than a delightful wedding. His thick black hair was longer than his brother's, he was a little taller, a little broader, and quite simply, to Juliet, a whole lot more…

He took a champagne flute from the tray, and whatever he said made the still-tense Susie briefly smile as he turned away.

His suit was the darkest grey, his tie a few shades lighter, and Juliet was filled with a sudden urgency for more detail. Not the salacious kind Louanna so freely gave away, but different details, like the sound of his voice, or the colour of his eyes, but he was too far away.

Deliberately she checked herself, looked at her music, tuned back into the world. Her slight absence had gone unnoticed, the music was sublime… But then she found her eyes drifting again, on high alert when she saw Sevandro was walking towards her.

Juliet's stomach clenched as it might have if the catch on a jaguar's cage had been unexpectedly released and the beast sauntered out. There was a sudden confliction, an odd acknowledgment of danger, and yet also a fascination that held her trapped for a moment as he walked towards her.

He was coming over, and so heavy was the pull, so dense the feeling low in her stomach, it seemed almost apt that he should acknowledge her. It took a couple of seconds for her to self-correct and register that rather than walking towards her, he was just moving in her general direction.

Of course…

She played on, unseen and unnoticed, watching from a safe distance as he approached the happy couple. Inwardly she scolded her own overreaction, watching his almost-scowl fade into a slim smile as he congratulated his grandfather and his glowing bride.

She looked away, tuning in to the music, and they were about to move into the second piece when Mimi announced, 'I have to sing!'

The musicians paused and, still a touch bewildered by her reaction to the very handsome stranger, still on alert, Juliet flushed with pleasure as the gorgeous diva came over. Mimi was the best form of distraction—and Juliet was utterly starstruck as she introduced herself to the quartet and asked everyone's names.

'"Una Voce Poco Fa",' she said. "A Voice I Once Heard" from *The Barber of Seville*.

Thank goodness Louanna had made sure they'd practised it.

It was truly a privilege to be there and to accompany Mimi. So much so that it allowed Juliet to put aside thoughts of the handsome widower as she played, revelling in Mimi's voice that moved like a swan floating on the water; the words so sensual, so seductive, it was as if Mimi was truly transformed into the flirtatious and spirited Rosina.

There was applause from their small audience afterwards, and a couple of 'Bravos!'—though of course they were for Mimi.

The ensemble played beautifully.

When a performance went well, it felt as if it was just the four of them, appreciating each other, meeting each other. Their instruments complementing rather than competing.

Their little squabbles forgotten, the hours of practice paying off as they barely noticed the hours flying by.

Juliet escaped into her music and almost forgot he was there.

Almost.

'We'll take a break,' Louanna suggested after a suitable time had passed.

But as Juliet put down her violin, stood and smoothed her dress, that aching awareness returned. Her head seemed to be fighting with her neck not to turn.

They were led downstairs into the main kitchen.

'Well done,' Cuoco the head chef at Pearla's congratulated them as they came in. 'Now it is my turn to take care of you.'

It was a sumptuous lunch, and they all fell on it. Performing really was hungry work at times, and today it was profitable too.

The event planner caught up with Louanna and handed her the pay envelopes. 'You're here till seven?' she checked, and Louanna nodded. 'Can you stay later if they ask?'

'Of course,' Louanna said.

'Did you bring concert dress?' the organiser asked.

'No,' Juliet said, worried she'd messed things up for the group, who had.

But Louanna wasn't letting this opportunity slip by. 'Can someone go out and get Juliet some make-up and black stockings?' she asked. She turned to Juliet and added, 'I have a bolero you can borrow.'

'Thank you,' Juliet said, looking at the cash figure on her envelope. She'd wear a bobble hat if they asked her to! The pay was so generous it meant that for the next couple of weeks she could breathe, as well catch up on exam practice without working at the bar to make her rent.

Thank goodness, she thought as she put her wages in her bag in the room under the stairs. But of course it was unsustainable; there wouldn't be many exclusive events like this. They really had lucked out.

Stepping out of the large cloakroom, Juliet was almost tempted to duck back in when she saw Sevandro—or rather, Sev, as his family seemed to call him—walking briskly past.

He didn't notice her—or more likely the Casadios were very used to staff—and he strode through the entrance hall, opened up a door and disappeared into a room, closing the door behind him.

Juliet stood for a second, wondering how the mere sight of someone could make her a little breathless. And why was she staring at the door he'd gone through and picturing him behind it?

What sort of force did he have that she wanted to walk over there? To go in...to see how he was?

How he *really* was.

It was no business of hers—nothing to do with her. But it was as if she could feel the tension behind that door and understood his need for a moment or two of escape.

It was the same with her and her own family.

Oh, her family surroundings weren't anywhere near as lavish, but she'd sat at too many family dinners, smiling and pretending everything was okay, or rather wishing it was... Wishing she could take things back and that she'd never repeated what she'd heard...

'Juliet?' Louanna had drifted up from the main kitchen with the others. 'Shall we go back in?'

'Sure.'

'*Scusi*...'

As they moved back to the dining room a male voice called to them and Juliet knew it was his. Deep and rather curt, it halted her, and yet she dared not turn. Instead, she left it to Louanna to take the query, and with Ricco and Dario went back to their instruments. Juliet felt too shy to speak, even in a professional capacity, terrified of blushing or stammering and making a fool of herself.

'We're staying on,' Louanna whispered as she joined them.

Sevandro returned to the dining room too, and took his seat at the large, polished table.

The afternoon session went well, and they took a supper break in the evening, when the family went to freshen up.

Having eaten, they prepared for the evening session—Ricco and Dario heading back quickly, having changed into jackets and bow ties, leaving the women to change.

As Louanna put on a long black dress Juliet pulled on the new pair of black tights and Louanna's bolero, then took out the make-up bag the organiser had sourced, unwrapping the lipstick—a very dark shade of red.

'I don't think my concert dress would have been up to the occasion,' Juliet admitted. 'I think it would look a bit faded for here.'

'That dress is too,' Louanna told her, in her oh-so-assertive way. 'Look at it compared to my bolero. You need to sort out your wardrobe.'

Juliet bit her bottom lip rather than respond. She might not like what Louanna had to say, but unfortunately she knew it was right.

Coiling her long hair into a chignon for a final touch,

she added the lipstick. 'How's that?' she asked, expecting another little telling-off.

'Sexy,' Louanna said, and Juliet laughed in surprise.

'Back to it,' she said.

It felt different.

There was no Susie to look out for—the caterers had gone—but there was a new feast spread out on the table, and there was whisky being drunk now, rather than Casadio wine...

Heavy jade drapes had been drawn the full length of the French windows, and the large dining room seemed to have shrunk in the darker, more intimate light. The guests were at the table, the older couple chatting animatedly, while the brothers were more muted, sitting opposite each other, both their chairs pushed back a little. It was as if they were leaning as far back from each other as they could.

The ensemble played quietly, all their favourite pieces. Sometimes a family member would look over and thank them, or suggest something, but really they were background music and enjoying being so.

Goodness, he was handsome, Juliet thought as Sevandro stood and wandered around, looking at the many family photos on display.

'It's a long time since we've done this,' she heard Gio comment.

'I was here in December.' Sev turned his head a touch.

'For a quick visit,' Gio said. 'You left before Dante arrived. We should get together more. I was thinking for the memorial we might...'

Juliet watched Sev's shoulders stiffen, his hand, holding a photo, go still. He was not looking around, but perhaps Mimi saw him tense too.

'Gio,' she intervened gently. 'Let's not discuss that today.'

It was as the night was winding down that the tensions started to rise. Mimi's sister left, and the newlyweds rose to see her out. Juliet didn't close her eyes as she played, but nor did she look at her music. Her eyes were drawn to the two brothers, alone for the first time today.

Neither said a word, but there was a certain arrogance to Sevandro as he poured himself a drink but didn't pour his brother one. Juliet was riveted, and found she could not pull her gaze away. She just stroked the strings with her bow, watching how the brothers stared across the table at each other, neither looking away and neither saying a word, the tension palpable.

Despite her outburst with Louanna, Juliet found she wanted to know more—wanted to know why the brothers didn't speak.

But there would be no answers tonight. In a slightly insolent gesture Sevandro pushed his half-empty glass across the table and made to stand. It looked as if he was about to go.

'Boys,' Mimi said as she returned. 'Stay.'

They might be boys to Mimi, but as the night progressed the air had become thick with testosterone, and Juliet wasn't sure that Mimi's suggestion to prolong the night was the wisest choice. There seemed to have been a slight loss of control in the carefully curated proceedings—or just a true glimpse of the Casadios when duty was done.

Juliet found that she rather liked it.

Louanna was applying rosin to her strings and Ricco was replacing one of his. She took a sip of iced water, the conversation from the table drifting over to her.

Mimi was lighting a cigarette and Gio was telling her off. 'Watch that beautiful voice,' he told her, even as he lit his own.

'It's my wedding day.' Mimi pouted.

'Dante?' Gio said. 'Are you able to visit the winery while you are here?'

'I can't,' Dante gave a curt shake of his head.

Gio sighed. 'Sevandro? How about you? How long before you head back to Dubai?'

Juliet didn't get to hear the answer as the music resumed, but soon there were more signs that Sevandro was leaving as he glanced at his watch. And as the quartet discussed the next piece, Juliet felt a curious sense of disappointment that soon the night would be done.

'Perhaps we could play one of Mimi's favourites?' Louanna was suggesting, flicking through music sheets.

Juliet's gaze drifted to the table. Gio was asking Dante why he hadn't brought a date to the wedding, but he declined to respond.

'And you?' Gio turned his attention to his eldest grandson, telling Sev he had a house, a home here, or surely he could stay at Dante's... 'And yet always you stay in a hotel.'

Sev put down his drink before responding. 'I might want to find company.'

'Then bring her along,' Gio retorted.

Only his voice seemed to be muted. And Juliet felt as if she'd stepped back into that soundproof booth. Because Sevandro Casadio was looking directly at her. For the briefest second it had felt as if he was addressing *her*, asking her a question...

She frowned, wondering if perhaps he had a musical

request, or was impatient for the ensemble to resume. With one look he imparted the heat of a thousand stars, made her too aware of her painted lips. Turning her gaze, she looked to her music sheet, then to Louanna, who gave her a nod.

The music resumed, the night went on, and really nothing had happened—except Sevandro's one blistering look.

Juliet's heart was pounding and she wasn't quite sure why.

It was an idle glance, she told herself. He'd been bored, just looking over, avoiding his grandfather's questions. And yet she found she kept wanting to look back and reclaim that moment. To meet his gaze again…to feel whatever she had briefly felt that second when she'd become aware of her red lips, for she'd been too aware of her mouth, had suddenly known how it felt to be absolutely held by eyes too far away for her to know their colour yet. Somehow, they'd held her riveted and still.

Juliet resisted looking over again, scared she would blush, or fumble her music. Surely the night was drawing to a close…

Mimi stood. 'One more!'

She came over to the musicians and Juliet saw that Dante rolled his eyes.

'Ah, I know…' She gave them a smile. '"O Mio Babbino Caro…"'

The musicians tensed, and Dante whipped his head up, but Mimi was oblivious, waiting for the music to cue her in. But they knew it was an aria that had been played at Sevandro and Rosa's wedding, and later at her funeral, and it was on the forbidden list.

Gio would surely halt this, thought Juliet, but he was

smiling at his bride, and now Juliet dared look at Sev. His expression was unreadable, almost impassive—if that word could be used to describe features carved from stone. But there was no emotion on display. He simply sat upright and very, very still.

What did they do?

The ensemble shared urgent glances, but Mimi was getting impatient, and Louanna made the decision to play, her cello leading them in.

Juliet didn't want to do it—she wanted to flee, watching in silent horror as Dante began to protest. But Sevandro gave a brief shake of his head to halt his brother.

With every stroke of her bow she felt as if she scraped it over his traumatised heart, but still he gave nothing away—not a single clue as to how he was feeling. He just sat through it, staring once at his brother, but apart from that he was clearly in his own head, alone.

Juliet wanted to put down her violin, but instead she played on.

She was torturing him.

To Juliet that was how it felt.

Sevandro didn't even flinch.

On the contrary, he applauded.

'Bravo,' he said as they concluded, and then applauded Mimi, before he stood and said he really must go.

He kissed Gio and Mimi…nodded in the direction of Dante.

Juliet did not get a second glance. She simply sat there, watching as he walked off while fighting the most ridiculous urge to run after him…

And she was fighting something else…something she didn't understand.

That company Sevandro had said he might want to find tonight…?

Juliet wanted it to be her.

CHAPTER TWO

'JULIET, THIS ISN'T what we agreed.'

It had been three months since Gio's wedding and Juliet was feeling even more behind with life... In an attempt to fix her finances and focus on her exams she'd responded to an ad on the noticeboard at the music school—free accommodation in return for a few light household duties.

Louanna had warned her she was making a mistake.

She'd been right!

'Anna, I said ages ago I wasn't available this weekend. I have a friend's wedding.' She shook her head. 'I'll be back in time to take the children to school on Monday.'

Juliet only had the hotel room for one night, but she badly needed her own space—this arrangement really wasn't working out.

She was flustered as she picked up her things. There could be no hasty exit with a violin case as well as her overnight bag, but at least her dress and shoes were already at the hotel, and Louanna had sorted out the music stands and storage of her back-up instrument.

Today the ensemble had another Casadio wedding to attend—and this one was going to be huge.

Juliet's instincts had been right. Susie was indeed pregnant. And on this sunny May day Susie and Dante were getting married.

It was such a relief to be out of Anna's and to walk into the heart of Lucca. From the day she'd arrived in the ancient city it had felt like home, and Juliet truly hoped that if work and visas worked out one day it would permanently be the case.

The hotel was old-world and elegant, and she felt a little underdressed in pale green cheesecloth and espadrilles, but then she realised the glamorous women and suited men might well be already dressed for Susie and Dante's wedding.

'Juliet Adams,' she said to the receptionist. 'I have an early check-in.' She couldn't help but ask, 'Are these people leaving for the wedding already?'

'Not yet.' The receptionist smiled. 'A few overseas wedding guests are meeting in the restaurant. It's an all-day event,' she explained as she tapped in Juliet's details. 'You have breakfast in the restaurant tomorrow. Oh, and I am to let the bride know when you arrive.'

Soon Juliet had her door key, an old-fashioned one, and she made her way to her room. She was just unpacking her bag when Susie arrived, dressed in a huge fluffy dressing gown, her hair all curled and pinned, delighted to see her friend.

'Oh, it's so good to see you. My sisters are driving me crazy.'

Juliet laughed, and hugged her, frowning when Susie handed her a pretty bag. 'What's this?'

'The underwear to go with the new dress that you wouldn't let us buy. Honestly, Juliet, you're part of the bridal party—you're my family here in Lucca.'

Juliet was touched. There was a unique loneliness to being in a foreign country when trouble hit, and that was possibly why Juliet had shared her financial woes and in turn Susie had admitted she was pregnant—oh, and then engaged, and now about to marry.

They sat on the bed and caught up. 'How was Dante with your family?' asked Juliet.

'They all seemed to get on. We'll see them back in London after our honeymoon.' She closed her eyes for a moment. 'The best man arrived very late last night.'

Juliet knew Susie meant Sev, though deliberately didn't react.

'I am a bit worried…' Susie admitted.

'Why?'

'You were there at Mimi and Gio's wedding. You've seen what they're like.'

'Not really…' Possibly the reason Juliet was so honest was that her very pale complexion flared red whenever she lied, but she attempted to lie now. 'I was too busy playing.'

'I'm surprised Dante asked him to be his best man,' Susie admitted. 'And perhaps more surprised that Sev agreed.'

So too was Juliet. She found she was biting her tongue in an effort not to delve, but Susie was anxious enough to fill her in.

'The one thing they agree on is that they both adore Gio. It would kill him if Sev wasn't there as best man. Even so…' Susie drew in a tense breath. 'Dante hasn't yet told Sev about the baby—that's why we've been keeping it quiet. Dante wanted his brother to hear it from him first, and he wanted to do it face to face.'

'But surely he'll be happy for Dante…?'

Juliet's voice faded when she thought of what Louanna had said. Usually she didn't probe, yet months on she still thought of that night and felt guilt-ridden when she recalled torturing him with her music.

'*Was* his wife pregnant when she died?'

'No.' Susie shook her head. 'Rosa wasn't pregnant. But…' She struggled to speak for a moment. 'When their engagement was announced Dante thought that she might be— The night before their wedding he suggested to Sev that Rosa might be trying to trap him. Dante's not exactly subtle. As you can imagine, it didn't go down very well.'

'No.'

'She wasn't pregnant. Dante got it all wrong. But he did have his reasons. There's more to it, but…' Susie's eyes filled with tears and she gave a helpless shake of her head. 'And now we're the ones marrying in haste.' She gave a mirthless laugh. 'Ironic, isn't it?'

'You two are crazy about each other,' Juliet pointed out. 'The baby's a bonus—not the reason for your wedding.'

They chatted more lightly, and Susie had cheered up by the time she left.

Juliet started to get ready—she had to be there well before the bride.

Pinning her hair up, and then applying neutral daytime make-up, she felt butterflies starting to flutter in her chest as she thought of the many guests that would be there today—and how important this was to her professionally.

She was about to slip on her dress, but then paused and took out the lingerie she'd been gifted, rather sure the delicate French lace wouldn't be enough support for her generous bust. She hadn't properly tried the bra on—she'd just been going along with things in the bridal boutique, and behind the curtain of the changing room she had barely done up the straps.

Juliet had only really guessed at her size—she'd always loathed bra shopping and her mother had been no help. Too busy with her new family and buying her own maternity bras.

Juliet could still hear her sigh.

'I never thought I'd be doing this again,' she'd said, flashing a look at her daughter.

Her father had said the same several times, when Juliet babysat for him and his new wife.

She'd felt the implication—*If only you'd kept your mouth shut.*

Some implications she might have imagined.

Others not.

'What did you think was going to happen, Juliet?' her mother had hissed. *'Of course you have to change schools.'*

And, no, she hadn't imagined her father's glare when he'd snapped, *'Why the hell do you think there's no money for violin lessons?'*

She did up the lacy bra, then pulled on the knickers and turned to the full-length mirror, still feeling as awkward as she'd been then. She looked at her pale body and rather fleshy bottom and stomach. The lace was so sheer she could see the pink of her areolae and nipples, and her hair was even redder *down there* and it showed.

Her phone rang and she saw it was Anna, but she was already nervous enough about playing and chose not to answer it.

She turned, about to reach for her own familiar underwear, but then hesitated and looked at her new dress. It had been a massive but necessary purchase. And because it was for work it wasn't as simple as just finding a black dress. She didn't like showing cleavage, especially when she was playing, and the arms had to be loose enough to allow movement, the skirt had to fall nicely when she sat…

She'd tried on several, and then the assistant had suggested this silky organza, way out of her price range. But the moment she'd slipped it on, Juliet had known it was perfect.

Now she felt the same, feeling the cool fabric sliding over her body, then doing up the concealed zip at the side. It looked better than she had remembered—the bias cut meant it fell beautifully, or was it the new bra that gave her a slight lift?

She slipped on her black shoes and took a seat in the dressing table chair. It was perfect. It didn't rise and show too much thigh.

She wasn't just being modest, worrying about cleavage and flashing too much thigh or worse… They were the last things she needed to distract her when she was playing…

Sevandro Casadio had distracted her.

The butterflies were still there in her chest, but she was aware of new ones too, fluttering low in her stomach.

They weren't the same, though. They were really an entirely different species. Because they didn't dart like the ones in her chest…they were subtler than that.

He'd be there today.

She'd thought of that when she'd first tried on this dress. She'd thought of him so many times since that night.

And now, even before she'd seen him, he was already distracting her. Her mind was darting with hope that they might talk, that she would find another piece of the delicious Sev or Sevandro puzzle and finally know the colour of his eyes.

Juliet closed her own—but not before she saw her cheeks turn an unflattering red.

She was blushing at the mere thought.

It was hopeless.

Sevandro knotted the pale pink silk tie—*not* one he would have chosen for himself—and had a word with his reflection in the large antique mirror.

'Best behaviour!'

Just get through this day.

These next couple of days.

No distractions, and no burying himself in work or women—which were his usual escape routes of choice.

He wasn't just here for the wedding—he was in Lucca to tie up loose ends.

This morning he'd been to the winery to check things were running to plan. Always he had a plan.

Patting his breast pocket, he checked for the rings—but for just a moment his hand hovered over his unexamined heart.

Just the wedding to get through, then a few detatils to sort, then one more trip for the ten-year memorial, and then...

He would be done with Lucca.

Catching sight of his reflection, he pushed out a smile. But the mirror confirmed it was false.

'Come on,' he told himself.

But the best he could muster was the businesslike smile that he might use when he greeted an investor or chaired a meeting.

It would have to do.

He took the gated elevator to his brother's suite, nodding to a couple who wished him good morning and asked him to pass on their best wishes to Dante.

They were, Sev was certain, talking about him before the lift doors had even closed.

Sev knocked on Dante's door and entered.

'Everything's under control,' Sevandro informed his brother, and gave him a few updates.

But their conversation was so forced it was a relief when Gio arrived.

'You're looking very smart,' Sev said as he let him in. The Casadio men were all wearing dark grey suits and matching ties. 'Where's Mimi?'

'Doing some vocal exercises before we head to the winery,' Gio said, and then looked at Dante. 'I thought I would come to wish you well.'

It dawned on Sev that Mimi might have stayed in her suite to give Gio some time with his grandson. Perhaps he should do the same?

'I might head down to Reception,' Sev said. 'Check on the vehicles.'

'Good idea,' Gio agreed. 'I'll be down shortly. Wait for me there.'

Gio did want to speak to Dante alone.

Sev took the ancient lift down and found a seat by a large column in Reception, silently strumming his fingers on the leather sofa, just a little out of the way of all the activity, shaking his head when offered a drink.

He was trying not to consider what Gio might be saying now.

God, but his parents would have loved to be here today. Two social butterflies, they would have been in their element.

Closing his eyes, he breathed in deeply, refusing to go there.

Just get through today.

There was the trill of a mobile phone, a slight scent of summer, and the feel of someone entering his space.

A cousin? An aunt? A family member of his late wife, perhaps?

Best behaviour, Sev reminded himself, feeling the indent of the sofa beside him as his company sat down, bracing himself to be told how he was feeling...how he must be missing Rosa today.

It wasn't that at all.

'Please, no...' someone said in English. 'Just leave me alone.'

She was speaking to herself, staring at her ringing phone, and she looked both gorgeous and familiar.

He watched her startle as she realised she wasn't on her own.

'Sorry...' She gave a nervous laugh and turned a shade more crimson than her reddish blonde hair. 'I didn't mean you.'

He said nothing, frowning a fraction, although not at the interruption. It was more that his slight frown was an invitation for her to explain. From Sev such an invitation was rare, but his recall of the stunning musician from Gio and Mimi's wedding was of someone sophisticated and poised, yet she was clearly flustered, blushing and clearly anxious now.

Why?

'My boss,' she explained, gesturing to her phone. 'She refuses to accept that I'm working today.'

'Your boss…?' he checked. 'Shouldn't she approve of you working on a Saturday?'

'No.' She shook her head. 'I have another live-in job.'

'I see…'

Juliet doubted that he did.

Furthermore, she doubted he wanted to hear about her dramas, so didn't elaborate. She would *never* have sat here if she'd seen him.

She assumed the conversation was over, gave an apologetic smile for disturbing him and looked away, back down to her phone. But she was still impossibly aware. Every nerve in her body had leapt to high alert, and now, for the first time, she was treated to his expensive scent—she hadn't been close enough before.

It did not disappoint. Subtle at first, spicy and peppery, but there was also a lower, woody note that made her breathe in a little more deeply, trying to define it. It was like night-scented tobacco plants after the rain…

Then he spoke. 'You were playing at Gio and Mimi's wedding.'

Somewhat stunned that he remembered her, even if she'd thought of him all too often, she turned and nodded.

He glanced down at her violin case. 'Are you playing this afternoon?'

'I am,' she agreed, and then, to save any possible embarrassment, quickly added, 'Though it's not just work. I'm also a friend of Susie's.'

'I won't be doing any speaking out of turn,' he said with an edge, clearly misconstruing her hurried warning.

'I didn't mean that.' She always left a conversation feeling like an incomplete Goldilocks, having said either too much or not enough. 'It's just better to say up front…given that I don't look like a wedding guest.' She gestured to her black dress. 'Somebody thought I was a guest at a funeral the other week.'

'Did they think you were the deceased's mistress?'

'Nothing as exciting. They did direct me to the viewing, though…'

He gave a soft laugh and she saw that his eyes were grey. But then she quickly looked away, simply pleased she now knew that much.

'So how do you know Susie?' he asked.

'We used to share a flat.'

'In England?'

'No, here in Lucca,' she explained. 'We hadn't met before that. I'm studying music.'

'Is your dreadful boss part of the ensemble?'

'No!' Juliet gave a small laugh, hesitant to explain, and positive that he was just doing his best man duty and being polite. 'It's all very boring.'

She had turned away again.

He glanced at the huge gold clock on the wall and wondered how long Gio's pep talk with Dante would last. What was being said?

She was now staring at her phone as if waiting for it to explode, and he realised he far preferred the distraction of their conversation to thinking about what was being said upstairs.

'Juliet,' he said, and she almost jumped at the use of her name. Two vertical lines appeared between her eyes and those lines were rare these days. 'You are allowed to turn it off.'

She had a beautiful unspoiled face. Her skin was as pale as porcelain—not just her face, but her bare arms and legs too. That was pleasantly unusual as well, and he wasn't thinking of olive-skinned beauties here—more those ghastly smelling spray tans.

'You could even block the number,' he added.

'That wouldn't be very sensible.' Her voice held a wry edge. 'I'm guessing you don't have a boss?'

'No,' he agreed. 'Well, I do have Sheikh Mahir. We're...' How best to describe that relationship? 'We're professionally intertwined, and he can be rather tricky at times.' Then he added, 'That's a polite way of putting it. And you're right—it wouldn't be very sensible to block him.'

He liked her gentle laugh.

Her phone bleeped again. 'Louanna,' she told him. 'The cellist. She messaged to say they'd soon be on their way, but now they're stopping for rosin.'

He frowned.

'For our bows. I'm sure she has plenty...she always does this...'

'Superstition?' he suggested.

'Maybe.'

And it dawned on her that Louanna might be nervous about today too.

It was then that the oddest thing happened. She realised she was no longer blushing. She took a breath and found it went all the way down to the bottom of her lungs, and that surprised her.

She'd thought she'd be blushing and dreadful if she spoke to him, and although she'd jumped out of her skin when she'd first seen him she felt more settled in his company now—if it was possible to feel 'settled' around someone as gorgeous as him.

Then she met his eyes and of course she was still a touch nervous—only not in the usual way.

They were more than grey. They were like a hail-filled sky with little glints of black and hints of a silver lining, as if the winter sun was struggling to appear.

She did not jerk her eyes away.

Those *other* butterflies were gently fluttering.

And they were curious.

'How do you know my name?' she asked.

'Probably the same way you know mine—that wedding went for hours,' he pointed out. 'And Mimi put in a lot of requests.'

'She did…' Juliet smiled with fond affection. Mimi had, of course, got to know all her accompanists. 'It was a wonderful experience.' And his confidence must be catching, because now she felt not so much bold, just assured in his company. Enough to ask, 'Do you prefer to be called Sev or Sevandro?'

'I answer to both.'

She liked both.

'And what do you do?' She knew about Dante's dazzling career, and Sev knew a little of her own, but she wanted to know about him. Not rumours, or scattered pieces put together. She wanted to hear from the source. 'You live in Dubai?'

'Correct. And, with the help of Sheikh Mahir, I used to purchase hotels. Now, though, we're looking to build a rather large one from scratch.'

'How large?'

'Over a hundred storeys.'

'Wow!'

'More than looking,' he added. 'We're in the procurement stage—pre-construction.' Now he asked a question. 'Are you looking forward to today?'

'Very much so!' She nodded, but then she saw he'd cocked his head slightly to one side, as if he knew that wasn't the entire case.

'Well, I will be once we get there. We're all a bit nervous—this wedding is the biggest we've done...' She halted abruptly. 'I probably shouldn't be saying this to a member of the bridal party.'

'Susie clearly thinks you're up to it.'

'Yes,' she conceded. 'Hopefully she's not being biased.'

'We've all heard you, Juliet,' he said. 'And Mimi isn't backwards in coming forward. She's singing today, God help us.'

'What?' She gave a shocked gasp. 'Her voice is stunning.'

'Is *your* step-grandmother an opera singer?'

'No.'

'That's why I get a pass to say it. She was also Gio's "housekeeper" for years.'

Juliet heard the quotation marks. Usually indiscretions unsettled her. They made her shrivel inside. And yet he spoke on, and she realised he wasn't being mean about Mimi's singing, or status, or anything like that.

He was reassuring her.

'I don't think our family are known for placating people. That includes Mimi,' he said. 'Her voice is incredible, and I know she takes it very seriously. If she wanted different accompaniment then she would have no qualms telling Susie.'

'Yes.' That helped—it helped a lot. 'She would.'

'So enjoy today.'

'Thank you.'

Juliet didn't understand how she could be in such stunning company and feeling so intensely attracted, yet somehow reassured, somehow starting to relax.

She hadn't felt any of these ways before.

These ways because there were many ways he made her feel.

It was just a conversation, one small part in his busy day, yet he gave her his full attention and it was like being placed under a gentle spell. She watched as he fiddled with his shirt collar, then checked his breast pocket.

'The rings,' he said. 'I'm getting like Louanna.'

It was a tiny joke, but it was one only they could understand. He too was nervous about today.

She wondered if Dante had told him about the baby yet, or if he was about to find out…

Then he saw her looking and she had to think of something to say.

'Your tie looks nice.'

'I'm not so sure—the bride chose it.'

Juliet was, for a nano-second, tempted to add that the bride had chosen her underwear, and she wasn't too sure about that either. Of course she didn't say that. It would be inappropriate and just a dreadful thing to say.

She settled for, 'Well, it looks very nice.'

'Do you want a coffee?' he offered as the eager waiter approached again.

'I'd better not. They'll be here for me soon.'

'A whisky to settle your nerves?'

'Gosh, no.' She smiled at his slight wickedness. 'Thank you, though. And for your company. I feel much better.'

Then she smiled at *him*.

* * *

She smiled from her plump pink lips right to her jade-green eyes, and for Sev it was as if her smile was a confirmation of what she'd just said.

There was no game, no flirtation, no attempt at seduction. Best of all there was no doubt as to its verity—it was a smile with no motive that came from such a rare place that, had his grandfather not called his name, Sev might, if he'd known how, have managed a real smile back.

One that said, *Thank you too for a nice moment on a hellish day.*

'Sev!' Gio called.

Sev didn't roll his eyes. Best behaviour and all that. But nor did he rush to a stand. He had one more quick question for her.

'Do I wish you luck or is that forbidden?' He thought for a second. 'Should I say *Break a leg*?'

'All good wishes are welcome.'

'Good luck then,' he said. 'And please…' He glanced down at her deliciously pale legs for the briefest second. 'Don't break a leg…'

Then he looked back up to hear her soft laugh and he did indeed smile. A smile so natural it remained even as Gio called his name again. It was there, even as he did now roll his eyes.

'I have to go and check on the groom…make sure he gets there on time.'

'What are you smiling at?' Gio asked as he approached.

'It's a wedding,' Sev pointed out, as if it was completely normal for him to be walking through this hotel lobby, smiling, when it was far, far from that. 'I'll head up to Dante.'

'Try not to fight.'

'Gio…' He wished people would stop banging on about it. 'That was years ago.'

'Just hear what he has to say.'

'Shouldn't I be the one giving the pep talk?'

'Of course, but weddings can bring out emotions…'

'Please,' Sev teased lightly. 'We both know I don't have any.' Then he saw the concern in his grandfather's eyes. 'Gio,' Sev reassured him. 'I'll take care of him today.'

'You are brothers every day,' Gio said. 'Yet the two of you talk like strangers sitting on a park bench.' He gestured to the couch Sev had just come from. 'If anything, you chat more easily with strangers…'

Sevandro took the elevator up to Dante's suite and was greeted by an immaculate groom whose nerves seemed to have caught up with him—he was pale and pacing as Sev poured the obligatory drink.

'Salute!' he said, handing his brother a heavy glass. 'How was Gio's talk?'

'He offered me a partnership in the winery.'

'You knew that was coming.'

'Yeah…' Dante looked at him. 'Look, I know it holds no interest for you, but while Susie and I are on honeymoon can you try and get back there? It's been neglected for too long.'

'Come off it,' Sev said. 'I was there this morning; it looks as if every last leaf has been polished. The place is stunning.'

He knew what Dante meant, though. The place had been beautifully managed and exceptionally well run by Christos since the accident, but Gio had seemed to age overnight, and since the tragedy his attention to detail had been lacking.

'It's managed fine without us all these years—just enjoy your honeymoon, as well as your time in England.' He tried to say the right thing. 'I know our parents would have been proud—'

'I know.' Dante cut him off.

Gio was right. They spoke like strangers. After all, he'd never even properly met the bride. How the hell did he know if they'd have been proud? Then he thought of them fondly and looked at his brother. Dante was in love and, yes, Sev knew for a fact they'd be both proud and happy.

'They would be,' Sev said.

Dante nodded. 'Before we head down…' He put his hand in his pocket and took out a black velvet pouch, which he handed to Sev.

'What's this?' He opened it up and inside found a thin piece of paper, folded many times.

'Are we doing drugs before you go down?' he joked.

'Open it.' Dante wasn't joking. 'You know how after the crash I hired a search party…?'

Sev said nothing. He did not want to think of that time, especially today.

Opening the paper he saw a small dark ruby.

'It's from Mamma's eternity ring,' Dante told him. 'They found two. I've never known what to do with them.'

'Did you show them to Gio?'

'God, no. It would finish him. I kept one for a gift for Susie. I thought you might want the other…'

'Perhaps give her this one too? You could have earrings made?' he attempted, just to get rid of the tiny stone that shone with memories. But Dante shook his head. 'Okay.' He pocketed it, not knowing what to say, steadfastly refusing to feel—he couldn't afford to today. 'Should we head down?'

'There's still plenty of time.'

'Even so…'

It was awkward. He'd far rather be on that couch, talking with Juliet, than standing here in a strained silence.

Dante broke it. 'Sev, I have something else to tell you.' He took a breath. 'Susie and I are having a baby.'

Ah, so this was the real reason for his brother's nerves.

'In October.'

'Congratulations,' Sev said, and met Dante's eyes. 'I'm pleased for you both.'

'I wanted to tell you first, face to face, but…' Dante spread his palms and the small gesture spoke of the abyss between them. 'I haven't seen you.'

'No.' Sev said. 'It's good news.' He smiled and raised his glass, but it was clear Dante didn't believe that was it.

'Just say what you have to!' he invited.

'Meaning…?'

'Whatever it is you're going to say, whatever wry comment you're going to make—just get it over with now.'

'Oh, no.' Sev shook his head. 'I'm on my best behaviour.'

'Oh, please…' Dante was disbelieving.

'I am,' Sev insisted. 'I am going to be the perfect best man. No smart comments…no chatting up the bridesmaids.' He put a hand on his brother's shoulder. 'I don't want the groom to black my eye.'

Dante gave a low, almost-laugh as Sev gently referred to yesteryear, then he looked at his brother and the faded silver scar. 'I am pleased for you.' It was the truth. 'I know that you, Mr Divorce Attorney, must love Susie very much. I knew at Gio's wedding it must be serious.'

'How?'

'You've never dated anyone who lives here,' Sev pointed

out—because, unlike himself, who had lovers everywhere, Dante only ever played well away from Lucca. His younger brother had always loathed the gossip here at home. And where the Casadio brothers were concerned there was always plenty. 'I knew if you were seeing someone here, then it must be serious. I'm happy for you, Dante, I really am.'

'Thank you.'

'Why so serious?' Sev checked, because his brother was still grey in the complexion and as close to tears as he'd seen him since the funerals. 'Dante...' Sev said. 'We fought ten years ago—move on from it. I have.' He spoke so assuredly Sev almost believed his own words. 'We're fine.'

They *almost* were.

Just as long as they didn't speak of that time.

As long as they remained in different countries and rarely got together.

'Today is your wedding day—let's not go over the past.'

It was everywhere, though.

It was there in the air they breathed, there as they drove in the car and passed the church, and the cemetery that housed Rosa's grave—which, to the scorn of many, Sev had never visited.

He did his level best to be there for his brother, trying not to compare the two wedding days, even managing a private joke as Mimi started to sing.

'Please, no...' Sev said, feeling his brother's silent laugh, as Mimi serenaded the groom. He knew Dante hated being sung to, because... Because they were brothers and he just knew.

Then Sev turned around and saw Susie approaching. And he was grateful that Dante had already told him about the baby because he'd have certainly found out now. She must be… He started to do the maths in his head, and then recalled looking at Rosa, whose pregnancy hadn't shown at all.

Stop, he told himself. *Don't compare, don't look back, just get through this day.*

'Your bride looks beautiful,' Sev told his brother, who now turned around.

'She does,' he said fondly.

And as she arrived by his side Sev saw there was so much love between them that, standing at the altar, he felt somewhat a spare part. Then he looked a little to the right, to the string quartet accompanying Mimi, and there was Juliet, playing her violin. Her eyes were closed and there was a slightly pained expression on her face. The same one he'd seen at Gio and Mimi's wedding, when she got into a particular piece. He'd been watching her that day too. How she swayed, how her left hand shook as she held a note…

There was tranquillity in the music, and the seemingly untroubled way she made it. She was back to being the woman he had first seen play…sensual and poised. Her red hair was almost gold in the sun, and her skin was so pale he found his eyes looking up to check there was adequate shade.

When the music stopped he watched as she rested her violin on her lap, her face flushed with pleasure as Mimi turned and thanked them. Then he watched as Juliet got her first proper glimpse of the bride, her mouth briefly gaping before breaking into a smile, and then she looked away from the bride and caught his eyes.

He gave her a small nod, to tell her just how perfectly she'd played.

* * *

Sevandro would never know how much that small gesture meant to her. Juliet had ached for it all her life—for that nod that told her she'd been heard and recognised. She was used to applause—it was part of her job—but to have that special nod was entirely different.

It was something she'd never known.

Not since she was twelve had there been someone there in the audience just for her.

Of course it was his brother's wedding, and from what she'd fathomed a difficult day for him, yet he made her feel special all through the proceedings. It felt as if he was looking out for her.

Of course he wasn't, Juliet told herself. He was best man, and it was his role to ensure things went smoothly.

As the guests mingled after the service with their aperitivos, and the quartet moved their equipment and instruments into the cellar, where the reception was being held, she saw him speaking with a waiter, and soon there were drinks and snacks waiting for them.

'Woo-hoo,' said Louanna, taking a long drink of sparkling water. 'For once we don't have to beg.'

It was a light tease, but all too often they were dashing to refill their own water bottles in the brief interludes.

'The cellar looks incredible,' she added, and Juliet too was taking in the scene.

It was one long table, dressed with incredibly tall candles. There were small posies of flowers, so as not to obstruct people's views, and the glass and silverware were stunning. It was a table prepared to enable conversation.

Like a ginormous family dinner, Juliet thought as they resumed playing and the guests drifted in to be seated.

The wedding feast commenced—and what a feast! Chefs from both Pearla's and the winery worked together and flamed huge cheese wheels to melt, tossing in fresh pasta beside the vast table, and it both looked and smelled incredible…

'We'd better get some of that when it's our turn to eat,' Louanna grumbled.

For now, they played, but that looked-out-for feeling remained with Juliet.

Occasionally she was aware of Sev glancing over.

Once, when she dashed to the ladies' room, he leant back in his chair as she passed. 'All okay?' he asked.

'Yes.'

He'd probably done the same with the others. She'd seen him speaking with all the staff. But this attention, this awareness of *one* other, was something she could not quite define.

When the guests started tapping their glasses for the bride and groom to kiss they obliged, and then there was a demand for Dante to speak.

'Grazie,' he said, thanking everyone for being there.

It was a very informal speech, more a call for people simply to enjoy, but then there were a few comments from guests about a *bambino*, and the secret was certainly out. As Susie stood, Dante kissed her, lightly touching her bump in a tender gesture that said there was nothing to hide, and everyone at the table applauded.

She found herself looking at Sev. His smile was perhaps a little tight, but he seemed relaxed in his seat. And then the guests urged him to speak.

Insisted.

Juliet felt her hands grip her violin a little more tightly.

She felt nervous and unsure why. Perhaps because Susie had been so worried about the brothers? Yet it seemed unfounded…the day was going beautifully.

Was Sev thinking about his wife? she wondered as he stood. Was he thinking about his own wedding day and what Dante had said all those years ago?

It would seem not. He was relaxed and fluid as he spoke. Juliet's Italian was good, but it was a little hard to hear him with the guests laughing and chatting and teasing.

'Zio Sevandro!' someone called, and a few others joined in, all calling him 'Uncle' Sevandro.

He gave a smile, though not like the one she'd seen in the lobby. Juliet frowned. Had she not seen his smile this morning, she wouldn't have known this one was forced.

'There is a lot of good news today,' he went on.

He was flawless, thanking the right people, toasting the stunning bridesmaids, saying how nice it was to meet Susie and see Dante so happy, how proud his parents would have been.

He was interrupted by a guest. 'And being Zio…?' the guest insisted, asking for his take on being an uncle.

Sevandro paused for just a second and Juliet waited for him to be the smooth best man and say something about the baby, or that he was looking forward to being an uncle. But he turned to his grandfather.

'Gio…' He raised a glass to the old man, who was smiling and dabbing his eyes. 'Bisnonno!' He called him Great-Grandfather, and Gio both laughed and cried as Sev once again mentioned his parents and how they would have loved this day, would have welcomed Susie.

Oh, the Italians loved a good wedding—and news of a baby too! They were all delighted.

Was she the only one who'd noticed that pause? Oh, Sev was impeccable, yet this *was* hard for him—Juliet somehow knew that.

The thought was confirmed when, at the end of his speech, he looked over to her.

It was Juliet who nodded this time.

It felt—although perhaps it was ridiculous—as if they were in this together.

Of course not...

The party commenced, and as more modern means of music replaced them they put their instruments away. Then, exhausted yet elated, the musicians sat down to their very own feast.

'Caspita!' Ricco exclaimed as, instead of a warmed-up meal, as was so often the case at this kind of function, Cuoco came to the table and they were treated to the same melting cheese display as the guests.

'Ah...' Louanna said, with a slight edge. 'We're in Casadio land now.'

Sev didn't make his way over, and throughout their meal he didn't once look their way. But Juliet could see him at the bar, his back to her, talking to various guests.

His attention on her had surely been her imagination... going into overdrive.

Yet as their dessert was served she asked herself why. Because when it came to men there had been no imaginings before. A few awkward dates, a handful of awkward kisses and some frantic attempts to relax as hands that felt unwelcome moved from her waist—whatever their direction, they'd always felt wrong.

'You're quiet,' Louanna observed. 'Are you worrying about the instruments?'

'I might go and check on them.' Juliet nodded, pleased to have a reason to excuse herself. 'I'll see if they've found somewhere suitable to put them.'

They had moved them to a safer storeroom than the one first suggested. Where to store their instruments at functions was a constant problem—the area they'd first selected had turned into a bit of a throughfare—but the wedding organiser had found a storeroom at the back of the cellar.

With the instruments all safely housed, she could now relax and enjoy the night. But instead of heading back to the table, or even joining the party, she used the staff exit.

Well, she was almost staff, and she was taking a small break.

It was her private thoughts she wanted to examine.

To work out what was happening.

If anything *had* happened.

Stepping out into the dusky night, she took a breath of warm air, listening to the muffled laughter and music from the party. Then, as her eyes grew accustomed to the dark, she saw a silhouette and recognised the broad shoulders.

Sev's back was to her, his posture straight as he looked out to the hills, but there was something in his stance that told her he'd needed a break from the happy proceedings too.

This day was hard for him—Juliet was sure of it. But, more than that, she rather guessed he'd prefer this moment to be a private one.

She quickly turned—just as the door clattered closed behind her.

'Juliet?'

'Hello.' She smiled. 'I was just…'

'Escaping?'

'Yes,' she admitted. 'You?'

She didn't expect an honest answer, but he turned around and in the inky night their eyes met.

'I guess I'm escaping too,' he said.

CHAPTER THREE

SEVANDRO GESTURED FOR her to join him, and she walked over, taking in the view, the darkness of the valley in the near distance, and beyond the twinkling lights of Lucca.

'I was just checking on the instruments,' she explained.

'Sounds like having children.'

'It probably is a bit like that at times.'

He looked down at her, but she could not hold his gaze and moved her gaze back to the view. She'd come out here to think of him and the tumult he caused in her head—which had somehow faded now she was by his side.

'You've been working hard,' he said. 'The music was incredible.'

'Thank you.'

'Are you finished playing?'

'I think so—unless someone asks.'

'You never did tell me about your terrible boss.'

'No...' Juliet gave a soft laugh as together they walked over to a heavy stone bench that looked out over endless rows of vines. 'I took a live-in job...free accommodation in exchange for a few household chores, babysitting, walking the puppy...'

'Free accommodation?' he checked. 'In my industry you'd need a fleet of staff for those *few* chores.'

'I get that now. Before that I was working a couple of jobs but falling behind at music school, as well as in rehearsals and practice. I've got exams soon—and a big thing in August.' She tried to offer both sides. 'In fairness to Anna—my boss—I have been getting more bookings for weddings. My weekends aren't as free as they were, and I don't think she understands just how much I have to practise. It's not the same with a practice mute...'

'Could you move?'

'I think I'll have to.' That was the only answer. 'I need a soundproof room—preferably on Mars.'

'Mars sounds nice,' Sev agreed, and somehow she knew he was speaking of escaping this night.

She wasn't a nosey person, yet it felt right to acknowledge that she knew he was a widower. Right to ask, 'Has today been hard for you?'

'I keep being told it must be,' he said with a sardonic edge. 'As well as how much I must be missing Rosa.' He turned and met her waiting gaze, and when he spoke again that edge to his voice was gone. 'You're the first person to actually ask.'

'You don't have to answer.'

'Thank you,' he said, then added, 'I mean that.'

They sat in silence for a moment, but then he said, his voice low, but a touch lighter. 'If I don't answer you, does it mean I can't ask anything about you?'

'Of course not.' She smiled. 'Perhaps let's answer only the questions we want to?'

'Sounds good to me,' Sev said. 'So, what happens in August?'

For Juliet it was the nicest question he could have asked.

'I'm going to be playing in the concert hall for five nights. It's an opera. I'm playing first violin.'

'Does that mean solo?'

'No!'

She liked it that he'd asked, that his eyes didn't glaze over as she told him about the different arrangements, how her dream was a permanent chair in an orchestra.

'Dante and Susie are coming to the opening night,' she told him—and his eyes still didn't glaze over. Instead they held hers steadily, and he was so receptive he made it easy to share the importance of her friends being there. 'It will make it extra-special. Don't tell them that, though,' she added. 'I don't want to add pressure.'

'Why would it add pressure?'

'If they knew how much it meant,' she told him. 'I've never had someone in the audience before.'

'Your family?'

'No.' She shook her head. 'They're busy, busy. You know how it is?'

'I don't...'

'Oh, I'm so sorry!'

Gosh, how insensitive of her, when his parents were dead.

But he smiled at her sudden anguish. 'When I was growing up my parents were always in the front row—much to my horror at times,' he elaborated. 'My mother liked to make an entrance and then she'd applaud just for me, and blow kisses.'

'Ouch!' She laughed. 'Did you play an instrument?'

'No.'

'Act?'

'I'm talking about little school plays. Thankfully we

went on to boarding school in Milan, or she'd have been embarrassing me through my teenage years too.'

He liked the softness of her laughter, and how it trailed away as if she understood how his parents were so greatly missed on this day. Then he reminded himself of his role as best man, and that his absence would soon be noticed.

As if to confirm it, in the distance his name was being called.

'I should get back.'

'And me. Louanna will be sending out a search party.'

They made no move to go, though.

And despite his promises to himself to behave on this day, now, at the eleventh hour, he caved. He wanted her tonight.

Sevandro stared into eyes that glittered and he liked the way she gazed back at him—as if anticipating the offer. But first there were clarifications to be made.

'So…' He resumed their conversation with different intent. 'No parents at your performances…what about boyfriends?' he checked, moving things along, aware that he had to get back inside and trying to gauge what this gorgeous violinist who had made today somewhat bearable expected from her lovers. 'Partners?'

'Gosh, no.' She shook her head. 'Nothing like that. I've never…' She shrugged. 'Well, what with my studies and…'

He assumed that, like him, she did not have the time or the desire for a serious relationship—but she was back to blushing, and his hand came to her burning cheek to let her know she did not have to apologise for preferring casual sex—certainly not to him!

'I guess with all that practice each day…' he said.

'And classes,' she added. 'There isn't time for dating.'

'Good—because I don't do all that.'

'I know you don't.'

She did know that—and right now it suited her.

Dreadful dates? They could bypass all that. They'd just go to bed.

And right now it didn't matter if that was it…

It was so much more than she'd ever had.

She wanted his skill and she wanted to be intimate with this man who had thrilled her on sight.

'You're staying at the hotel?' he checked.

She nodded.

'I'll sort out a key,' he told her. 'But now I should go.'

Juliet frowned, expecting a kiss.

Usually she felt a little fearful at this part…never quite wanting the kiss that was to come.

This was the complete reversal of that. He just stared. And her lips ached as if they needed the weight of his. And she had never stared at another so intently…

Then she heard his name being called once more, and she could have wept.

'They can wait,' Sevandro said, and she felt a flutter of relief as his mouth came down and lightly grazed her own. 'First I have to know your kiss.'

And she got to know his.

It was bliss, light and yet sexy, as if she were being brushed by velvet, and yet it set off a delicious reaction, from her tingling lips to her toes. As his hand slid behind her head she was shaking—but with pleasure. His mouth exerted more pressure and her lips parted to the reward of his tongue.

This was how every kiss should be.

It was slow, unhurried, and she closed her eyes and wondered why she'd been so reluctant in the past—why she'd fought not to pull away, and yet with Sev she instinctively moved closer.

She put her arms up and wrapped them around his neck. He kissed her harder. But what brought her undoing was the sound he made in her mouth…almost a sigh, akin to a moan. A sound more beautiful than any her violin could make.

His lips on hers were no longer soft, but thorough and delicious, and she kissed him back, their tongues mingling and her body all atremble as his hand came to her waist and he drew her closer.

Sev did not generally sit necking on a bench, and he hadn't intended to kiss her here, but this was a delight. And, while he was aware he had to go inside and resume his best man duties, he knew there was so much pleasure that awaited and this taste would sustain him.

He took her hand and moved it to where he ached, groaning at her teasing as she moved it to his thigh. His mouth explored her pale neck and he kissed away the throaty noises she made, knowing he must go.

But first he had one more question.

'Why did you deny me?'

'Deny you?'

'That night, why did you deny me?'

'Deny…?' she said again.

He heard the bewilderment, felt the pause in her body. He was about to insist she knew what he meant—and then it was he who stilled.

It was Sev who halted this tryst.

He went over her words, felt her hand still on his thigh…

She hadn't denied him that night.

He was starting to realise Juliet hadn't known that, when he'd told Gio he might find company for the night, his look had invited *her*… She had flicked her gaze away, and at the time he'd thought he was being given a very sophisticated no.

But she was a different woman with her violin.

The real Juliet did not know this game.

She didn't know anything!

'When you say you've never dated?' he checked. 'Are you telling me that you've never slept with anyone?'

'Yes. But I know my mind, Sev. It doesn't change anything between us.'

'Of course it changes things.' He dropped all contact. 'What the hell, Juliet? You are not into one-nighters.'

'You don't know that.'

'I do know that,' Sev said. 'Because I've already offered you that.'

He saw the furrow form between her brows.

'At Gio and Mimi's wedding.'

'We didn't so much as speak…' she started—and then her lips closed.

Juliet swallowed as she looked back with hindsight.

That look that had caused her heart to race…that moment when she had felt as if he spoke directly to her, as if he had a request…

Well, he had.

Just not the musical kind.

'Did you really think I was just going to finish playing and go to your bed?'

'If you so chose.' He took a breath. 'Don't you see? It's the same tonight.'

'No!'

She wouldn't have it. It wasn't the same. They'd connected, they'd spoken, they were talking now!

'Sev…' Juliet was struggling, trying to regroup from the bliss of their kiss and the promise of the night and then the plunge into rejection. 'I know we're not going anywhere, but I do know what I want.'

'*Do* you?' he checked, a little less gently, perhaps tartly. 'Because I don't do slow and tender, and I don't make love.'

'I'm not asking for love. I'm not expecting to be treated as if it's our wedding night. And I never said I wanted "slow and tender".'

'That,' he snapped, 'shows how little you know.'

'Why does my being a virgin scare you off?'

'Oh, I'm not scared, Juliet. I'm more concerned that we'd have got into that room and I'd have taken you against the wall…' He quickly shut that thought down. 'Juliet, what do you want for your first time?'

She stared angrily back at him. 'Preferably someone who turns me on.'

He gave a small laugh at her smart answer, because there could be no denying their ridiculous attraction, and he was kinder when he spoke again.

'Be honest, Juliet, in an ideal world, what would you want from your first lover?'

'I don't want to answer that one,' Juliet said. After all, that was the agreement they'd made.

'You do *not* want to cut your teeth on me.'

'Please don't tell me what I do and don't want.'

She stood and smoothed down her dress and he stood too.

'Your hair…'

He put a hand to her head to smooth it, and he was so nice as he sent her on her way. But then she answered his question—not to satisfy his curiosity, just to remember how she'd once thought.

'I do want more for my first time. I don't mean endless love—but, yes, red roses and such…and to be wined and dined…to dance and…' She halted.

'Go on.'

'I want someone who knows parts of me that no one else does, and gives me parts of himself…'

He was right, damn him.

'What else?' he asked.

'Picnics in sunflowers.'

'Picnics are muddy and itchy.'

'It's my dream, Sev.'

'Hold on to it,' he told her, and then he gave a soft laugh. 'Picnics? Oh, Juliet, you really did pick the wrong guy.'

'So you keep telling me.' She sniffed. 'I'm going back inside.'

She nipped to the ladies' and sorted out her hair and splashed her face, then headed back to the wedding. It was a gorgeous night, utterly perfect, and yet seeing Susie and Dante dancing, and all the other couples—some together for ever, some just together for this night—she felt out of step with the world.

'Come on,' Ricco said, and so they danced. Because they liked music and that was that.

It would have been nice to make Sev a little bit jealous,

but there was no chance of that, because Gabriel came to grab his hand and Ricco was back dancing with the one he'd be with tonight.

She caught Sev's eyes and rolled her own, then got back to life without him.

'Juliet!' Susie was high on hormones and love. 'Thank you…'

'I've loved every minute,' Juliet said. 'It's been wonderful.'

It really was a brilliant wedding, and she danced some more, and then sat with Louanna, debating whether to play some music as the night wound up.

'There's a fire pit outside,' Louanna said.

'I can't take my violin by a fire.'

'Use Ricco's old spare?' she suggested, then paused. 'God, they could at least be discreet.'

'Who?'

''Sevandro and Ella,' she said. 'She's *married*!'

'They're just talking,' Juliet snapped, more than a little fed up with Louanna's well-voiced opinions—though it did sting a little to see Sev in conversation with a stunning caramel blonde. 'Let's get the instruments.'

Sev saw Juliet heading outside—or rather was aware of her no matter how he tried not to notice.

That kiss still lingered in his mind, and also their conversation, and the music she'd made…

All the good parts of today, the gentler parts of today, had been because of her.

Damn.

He really hadn't handled things well—but then again, since Rosa's death he hadn't been one for sitting outside at night and looking at the view, or talking and making out on a bench.

And he wasn't one for virgins.

'Am I boring you, Sev?' Ella said.

'I'm sorry…' He pulled his mind back to the conversation.

'It's okay. I know today is hard for you.'

Juliet had *asked* if today was hard for him, rather than assumed it was. Ridiculously, he had wanted to discuss it with her, but he had closed off that escape hatch years ago.

'You must miss Rosa today…'

He chose not to respond to Ella's assumptions, and instead asked after her husband and young family.

'They're doing well. Of course we're busy…both working.'

'You took over the practice?' he checked. 'How is your father?' he asked.

Because there was a part of him that still wanted to speak to the older Dr Romero. A part that did want to know if his suspicions—Dante's too—had been right.

If there had ever been a baby.

'I was thinking of maybe visiting him,' Sevandro said. 'Just to catch up.'

'He'd have loved that, Sevandro, but he's not so well.' Ella told him about her father's dementia. 'It's so hard to lose a little more of him each day, and visitors just confuse him.'

'I'm very sorry to hear that.'

'He adored both you and Dante. The sons he never had.'

'Give him my best.'

'I will,'

As Ella slipped away he got back to duties, arranging

the wedding car, and everyone stopped to wave off the happy couple.

'Give England my love,' he heard Juliet call as they climbed into the car.

And then she got back to the fire, playing her violin like a fiddle, and making people happy with the music she made.

The music was happy—the musician not so much.

Oh, it had been wonderful, and she loved nothing more than playing with friends like this, but she wanted to go back to the hotel and lick the wounds of her rejection.

Juliet saw him leave.

Not a moment after the bride and groom had gone, Sev signalled for a vehicle and without so much as a backward glance left the reception.

The party carried on, and so did the music, but after an hour or so Juliet gave in, returning Ricco's violin, collecting her own, and then climbing into one of the waiting cars.

It was a lonely ride back to the hotel—and Juliet was more than used to it.

Not so much returning to a luxurious hotel, more the wired feeling from performing. But tonight it was heightened. Or was it that she was still wired from that kiss? Or that delicious time spent on the bench, simply talking?

She stepped into the gorgeous foyer, almost drooping—not with weariness, but with dejection—and a head full of faded long-ago dreams of men who dated you and the shining star of one who didn't do that at all.

'Allow me.'

The doorman spoke in Italian, and so lost in her thoughts was Juliet that it took her a second longer than usual to translate as he reached for her violin case.

'I shall have it delivered to your room.'

'No need,' Juliet responded. 'I can manage.'

She walked off, past the sofa where they had spoken this morning, wistful and a bit misty-eyed as she waited for the elevator. She would like to get to her room and cry, Juliet decided. Although she was unsure if she was embarrassed at practically handing herself to him, or simply sad that he'd turned her down.

There was no sense of feeling relieved that nothing had happened.

Turning the old-fashioned key, in the equally old-fashioned lock, she realised the simple fact was she was tired of being considered an old-fashioned girl.

Juliet had wanted him so.

The lights were on as she stepped into her room, but instead of putting her violin case down she stood holding it, a little stunned, staring at the floral arrangement—deep red roses wrapped in gold paper—that had been placed on the dressing table.

Oh.

They must be from Susie, she told herself. Because she was nice like that.

Her heart started thumping as she put down her violin, then walked over and picked up a cream envelope with spiky black writing on it: *Juliet.*

She almost tore the envelope in her haste to get to the card, expecting her hopes to be dashed, and let out a sob when instead hope was renewed.

Before making love, at the very least he should send flowers...

Sevandro

Her breath was rapid and shallow, making her a little dizzy as she reread the card and then looked back inside the envelope. She took out a little flat numbered card and saw it was a lift pass.

And with those flowers he took her back to something that had never been, to her dreams for her first time, how it might be, should be…

Could still be.

She inhaled the scent of the roses and marvelled at how he'd got hold of them at this hour. She didn't know—she just knew that it was the single most romantic thing he could have done.

It made tonight special…

She walked into the bathroom and wondered how to prepare. She took in the shower, the deep bath, her tiny make-up bag… There was no time. She wanted every minute of this fading night to be spent with him. So she freshened up quickly, added a little lip gloss, then took down her hair and quickly brushed it.

Her nerves crept up as she used the card to access the elevator and it slowly creaked its way up. Oh, so badly she wanted to do this—to spend a night with Sev—but as she exited the elevator and stood at the door she didn't know *how* to do this. How to knock on his door and say, *Hi, I'm here…*

Hating herself for being so pathetic, she turned to go, summoning back the lift, hearing it groan as it wearily returned.

'Juliet…?' Sev was peering out through the door.

'I think I've got the wrong floor,' she lied.

'This is my floor,' he told her. 'And the only way to get here is the private access card.'

'Oh.'

'No problem.' His jacket was off, his tie unknotted, and he looked more delectable every time she saw him.

'Goodnight, then,' he said.

'Is this really your floor?' she asked.

Sevandro nodded.

God, he thought, she was nervous.

Usually it didn't endear him to a woman, but then again, he'd never taken such time with a woman before. He rather guessed she'd hate herself tomorrow if she left now. And he'd regret it too. She was sexy as hell and just didn't know it. He'd felt her desire on the bench—perhaps because she knew it couldn't really go anywhere.

'It's okay,' Sev told her as she walked back to his door. 'It's a first for me too.' He took her in his arms. 'I've never slept with a virgin.'

There were questions in her eyes that he would not be answering. He did not want to discuss a long-ago wedding night that had been tense rather than tender.

It had not come close to this.

Tonight was no longer about distraction—and for him sex was usually that: an escape or a need fulfilled. He had lovers he could call—beautiful women who, like himself, did not want to tangle emotions.

This wasn't like that.

First, though, she had to relax.

'I have to make some calls,' he told her.

'I'll go…'

'No, I meant if you want to have a bath… I have to call my PA in Dubai.'

He led her into his vast suite. The doors were open to

the balcony and that massive moon was still hovering, as if it had followed them from the vineyard. She'd seemed so much bolder there.

'I arranged this for you.' He opened up a door and she looked at all the candles and the steaming water.

'You did this?'

'The maid did it. I'm sorry I can't wine and dine you, but Italian weddings...'

She laughed, and it was nice to see her relax just a touch.

Sevandro had thought a bath might be good for both of them, and though he had since decided she might feel better alone he did not want that bathroom door closed. Very deliberately he would maintain the contact.

'We could have breakfast tomorrow,' he said as she went into the bathroom.

Hopefully she wouldn't still be a virgin by then, Juliet thought as she slipped into the bathroom.

She was about to close the door, but then he called out, 'I didn't know Susie's sisters were twins.'

'Yes.'

She kept on trying to close the door, but he had more to say.

'They didn't like all the attention being on Susie.'

'No.' She smiled, undoing her zip. She'd noticed the same.

'Do you have brothers and sisters?'

'Half-brothers and sisters.' It was nice to talk as she took off her dress and stood dressed only in French lace. 'All much younger. My parents got divorced.'

'How old were you?'

'Twelve when they broke up.'

He wasn't listening now.

'Helene?' he said. 'Thanks for getting back to me…sorry to call you at this hour…'

He rattled on about Sheikh Mahir and Juliet took off her underwear and slid into the bath and lay there, worried now rather than nervous. Leaning over, she looked at her phone and found out it must be three in the morning in Dubai.

Now she had a question of her own.

'Sev?' she asked when he'd ended his call.

'What?' he replied, coming to the bathroom door holding a drink.

'Do I smell?'

He laughed. 'Why do you ask?'

'Well, putting me in the bath…pretending you had to call Dubai…'

'I did have to call to Dubai. But to be honest I thought you needed a bath to relax. I'm not one for…'

'What?'

He came over and sat on the edge of the bath. He picked up her hand. 'Oh, Juliet…' He kissed her fingers, mimicking being chaste. 'I'm not one for feeling my way slowly…'

'It's nice, though,' she said.

Especially when he stopped faking being chaste and put down his glass, focussing on her hand and sucking on one finger. Then he paused, his silver-black eyes looking at her.

'Your underwear is very sexy.'

'The bride bought it for me.' She could tell him that now. 'Like your tie.'

'Seriously?'

She nodded.

'Why?'

'She just did.'

'I cannot think of a single occasion when anyone would buy me underwear.' He thought about it. 'And I would never buy it for anyone…'

'You don't buy your lovers sexy lingerie?'

'God, no, I don't do gifts.' He kissed up her arm. 'You lucked out again,' he said, kissing her neck. 'You got a mean billionaire.'

'You're not mean…'

No man with a mouth so soft on her neck could be called mean.

'Selfish, then.'

His hand came to her gorgeous breast, floating in the soapy water. Pulling back a little, he looked at her, huge black pupils with just a dash of green at the edges and her hair all curly from the steam.

And when he kissed her softly, Sev knew he'd never before come close to this moment. Feeling her tentative mouth, he made allowances for it, didn't try to hasten her with his tongue.

He'd never kissed like this—had never wanted or even needed to take the time to reassure a woman.

But Juliet suited his mood now, and as his tongue slipped into her warm mouth his hand moved between them, stroking the side of one generous breast. Her hardening nipple, despite the warm water, felt like a reward.

His hands, his mouth, felt incredible.

'I've wanted you since this morning,' he told her in a low, gravelly voice that made her feel both weak and wanting.

She started to unbutton his shirt, exposing the fan of

black hair on his chest and flat mahogany nipples. He was just so male, so sexy…

He sat on the edge of the bath, so tall. Then he shrugged off his shirt and lowered his head, taking one breast in his mouth as his hand slid lower.

'You might fall in…'

'I don't care.' His tone was emphatic.

His hand was between her thighs, his fingers where none had ever been, and then his mouth left her breast, as if he preferred to look right at her.

Her hand moved to his shoulder, and then to the back of his head, and she stared right at him, closing her eyes at the slight stab and stretch of his fingers before they moved back to soft strokes.

Strokes that were more insistent.

'I don't think I can come,' she told him. 'Why don't we…?'

'Shh…' he said, concentrating on the feel of her, beneath the soapy water.

Then her hand came to caress his face.

Her warm, tender touch was almost too much for his black, icy heart, and yet he found he coveted it.

He looked right at her, feeling her come alive under his hand, seeing the flush on her cheeks and the slight sheen of tears in her eyes. He breathed in. He wasn't just turned on as he watched her come to orgasm, feeling her thighs grip him and her intimate beat—he felt something scarcer… felt a deeper contact being made, someone being with another. Caring…

'Sev…'

She closed her eyes, folded a little in the middle. He leant forward and she rested her head on his chest, his dark hair against her cheek, and his hand moved up to her waist as the pulses faded.

'I didn't think…' She was struggling to get her breath. 'I didn't think I was capable…'

Nor had he.

For ever he'd been numb.

Well, at least for a decade.

But now, as they lay on the bed, naked and kissing and aching for each other, touching each other, stroking each other…

'Let me…'

She was nipping at his nipple, then asking if it was nice.

'Yes.'

Her hand was on his stomach now and, nervous but bold, she slid it down. They lay face to face but he was looking down, watching her stroke him.

'I should put something on,' he suggested, as her fingers were moistened with his silver.

But they were both watching, and her breasts were warm, damp…just so nice to explore with his hands and with his mouth.

He was about to hook her leg over him and drive in, but…

He had to take it slow.

He liked her hand on his back as he reached over to the bedside table, rummaging for a condom, knocking the contents off but not caring.

He liked how she slid her hands between his thighs as he briefly faced away from her.

He rolled onto his back. 'Put it on me.'

'You do it.'

* * *

She watched him for a moment and then she took over, her slender fingers rolling it slowly down. She looked at Sev and leant over and kissed him. He pulled her head down and kissed her back hard, his jaw a little rougher now, and that giddy feeling was back as he flipped her and kissed her, removing a pillow from beneath her head.

The feel of him over her was delicious, and so was the scratchy feel of his thighs between her legs as he positioned himself. He was focusing on her neck, and then he moved up onto one forearm, holding himself at the centre of new pleasure.

'Sev...'

She was so ready she was almost begging. As he pushed in she waited for the hurt and pain, but it was more just a new and blissful sensation.

'Oh...'

The room went a little dark, but then there was nothing but pleasure, and the ragged moans from him made her curl inside.

'Juliet...' he said, almost as if he was apologising, and then he started to move.

She was so oiled and ready, so in tune from their long games in the bath, that it was new but not scary.

'Okay?'

He looked down from over her and their gazes locked. She nodded to say that she was okay and he moved deeper.

'It's perfect.'

She searched for his mouth and kissed him as he took her, her hands finding the planes of his back and moving down to his torso.

She lifted her knees and then wrapped her legs around

him. He was moving faster, and she tasted his shoulder, his chest, wanting this never to end. But she could feel heat spreading, and there was the same warm feeling she'd had in the bath, except there were no little beats of pleasure, just a build-up of tension.

She started to moan, as if seeking escape. Then he stilled, and a zip of electricity seemed to shoot along her spine as she heard him moan and release. It was the headiest pleasure, her face on fire, her throat tight, but nothing like the tension and the intensity of her orgasm as he came inside her.

His head came down beside her own, and then he lifted a little and moved within her again, where she was so tender, before collapsing on her.

Juliet had nothing with which to compare, but she simply knew, as she lay there warm with pleasure, that somehow she could only have been found by him. As if since he'd laid his sexy eyes upon her that first night they'd been building to his, and now she lay sated and breathless as he moved from within her.

Sev sorted himself and then covered them. He waited for the moment to arrive when he wished she were gone, or for that numb feeling to return, but his new lover didn't allow for that. She was lying over on his side of the bed, her hair on his chest, and clearly delighted.

'That was magical,' Juliet said. 'Honestly, how did I survive without that?'

She leant over him to get some water and he felt her hair trailing over his face. It didn't annoy him.

'Sev…?' She was suddenly very still over him. 'You didn't take anything, did you?'

'What?'

He glanced over, saw the little sliver of paper and couldn't resist a little tease.

'Dante gave it to me before the service.'

'Dante?'

He laughed and reached over. 'It's a precious stone.' Unwrapping it carefully, he showed her the contents. 'A ruby.'

'Oh.'

'From my mother's eternity ring.'

His smile dimmed. He'd almost refused to look at it when Dante had given it to him—really, he'd given it only a mere glance—but now he held the little stone up to the light.

'Dante had it recovered from the accident site.'

'Now I feel terrible…'

'No need.' He folded the ruby back inside the paper and into its pouch, then put the little package in the drawer 'There's nothing terrible about tonight.'

CHAPTER FOUR

'I WAS RIGHT,' Juliet said, lying with her head on his chest, tethered by his arms.

It was just as well, because she felt so relaxed and floaty that she thought if he let go she might just float away.

'About what?'

'My first time was perfect.' She thought for a moment. 'Well, I didn't get a picnic...' She both felt and heard his low laugh. 'Or a dance. But apart from that...'

There was another thing she'd asked for, to share pieces of themselves only with each other, and perhaps that was why she asked now, 'Was your first time this romantic?'

'No!' He half laughed, but then lay still, thinking back to a version of himself he had long since forgotten.

For so long it had felt as if his bastioned life had started after the accident, or the fight with his brother, or his marriage. But this rare togetherness with another person, the curiosity rather than nosiness behind her question, meant his perpetual guard didn't shoot up. Her gentle silence allowed him to think.

'It wasn't like this, but perhaps it was a bit romantic.'

'Was it her first time too?'

He shook his head. 'She was older...a tourist.'

Juliet's questions still didn't feel invasive, even if it was something he had never discussed with anyone. Even if it was a topic that might be best not discussed as you lay with another woman. There was an honest element to her questions, and the agreement they'd made that they didn't have to answer—it made it easier for him to explore the past.

'She was staying at Forte dei Marmi...'

He told her about the sandy beaches, the jet-set tourists and luxury hotels...

'She was there for a few weeks. It suited us both...' He thought back. 'I was never in love, or anything like that, but I thought she was incredible. We both knew it was short-lived.'

'A holiday romance?'

'For her. I wasn't on holiday—I was working. For me, it was more a short indulgence.'

He thought back to lighter days. He'd always been serious, and held back from getting overly involved, but that long, hot summer was a world away from the brief interludes he allowed himself now.

'I was probably better company then.'

'I like your company now,' she told him. 'And I can see the appeal of short, intense relationships. It doesn't have to be for ever to be wonderful.'

Her words struck within him, making him think of long-ago days when he'd never given his heart or made promises he'd never keep.

'You're right...' He looked down, saw they were loosely holding hands. 'It doesn't have to be for ever to be...'

He couldn't say it. He didn't do 'wonderful' and never had. He'd always been a bit of a lone wolf, and more cynical than most, but there was something about lying here with her, the day he'd been dreading since his brother had told him about it now safely over.

'To be incredible,' he said.

Incredible because for more than a decade all his emotion had been locked in a vault, and tonight he had allowed himself to feel, to make love, to hold and caress and just escape into her charms and her scent. To get to know her some more.

For Sev, *that* was sheer indulgence.

'How old were you?' she asked.

'That, I am not answering.'

'You were old enough to work, though?'

'Work experience.'

'No-o-o...' She moaned and covered her face with her hands.

He leant forward and peeled them from her face. 'That was the same as most of my relationships.'

'With holidaymakers?'

'Yes.' He hadn't ever really thought about it, but now, looking back, he saw it. 'We could be close, but there was an expiry date. I could adore them, but know it wasn't going to last. It worked both ways—both of us knew the terms.'

She didn't seem shocked. 'Actually, it sounds perfect.'

'I think you might have more heart than me.'

'No...' She lay still. 'I wanted this—honestly. I really don't have time for a relationship. I have the most important months of my life coming up. I need to concentrate on that.'

'Why did you wait?' he asked. 'And don't give me all that nonsense about being too busy.'

'It's true, though,' she said. 'Well, in part... I told you my parents broke up when I was twelve, then both married again. I was always being roped in for babysitting and then I was working to pay for my music lessons.'

'They didn't pay for them?'

'Things changed after the divorce. School…their finances…' There was a stretch of quiet. 'We don't get on. Of course we never actually *say* that, but…' She trailed off, as if she was skipping past something. 'Then I went to university and I honestly thought my life would start then—well, dating and such. But…' She stopped again. 'You've never been shy, I assume?'

'Shy?' He thought about it. 'If you mean timid, then no. But I wouldn't say that about you either. You perform, you dance, you have friends…' He shook his head. 'Being busy is an excuse.'

'We can't all dive into bed with a single look.' Juliet thumped his chest, but then sighed.

They lay quietly and Sev wanted to know more—he wanted to get to the bit she'd glossed over. But that wasn't fair. They'd agreed not to press each other.

It was still there, though, that desire to talk…to open up to her.

They dozed, and she awoke lying on her stomach, felt herself being watched.

She smiled right into his eyes.

'You're not shy,' he told her.

'I'm not shy with you,' she admitted. 'Or maybe it's my casual lover persona?'

'Do you want breakfast? We could have it here or go down.'

'I'm not sure… I think the hotel restaurant might be a bit

public. I'm not slinking about, but…' She rolled her eyes. 'I'd prefer it if Susie didn't know about last night.'

'Fair enough.'

'She'd be arranging double dates.'

'God, no,' he laughed.

'Oh, yes. And, knowing Susie, she'd have us seated together at the christening.'

His smile faded.

'I was joking, Sev.'

'I know that… You and Susie?' he asked. 'You're very close?'

'We are.' She leant up on her elbow. 'Though I shan't say anything to her about this. We're not *that* close. I don't normally open up to people.'

'I believe you.'

'And, given I don't discuss my sex life—or lack of it…' She looked right at him. 'I don't like to get too involved with anyone either.' She pressed her lips together for a second before continuing. 'Believe me, I shan't be saying anything about…'

She gestured to the rumpled bed.

'I don't mind,' he told her.

He put a hand up to her gorgeous hair.

No, he decided, she wasn't shy. It was something more.

And if he wanted more of those pieces of her then he should give her some of his own.

Some of those things no other person knew.

'Yes,' he said suddenly, and watched her slight frown. 'In answer to your earlier question, yesterday was hard for me. Thank you for being there.'

She smiled, and he looked at the jade-green eyes that

were so patient, and he felt he was on the edge of telling her something not a single soul new—answering the second assumption all those others had made, that he'd missed Rosa yesterday.

'As to the other… No.'

She gave a tiny nod, the same one they'd shared a couple of times yesterday, and he knew she was just understanding that this was hard, and offering support.

'I didn't miss Rosa yesterday. I am sad that she died, but our marriage wasn't as good as everyone believes.'

'I'm so sorry…it must be hell whenever you come back here.'

'Yes.'

'Do you see her family?'

'They were there last night. They're always there. They own a small winery next to ours.'

He inhaled deeply. *Enough.* He looked over, wanting something in return.

'Who hurt you?' he asked.

'No one.'

But he knew that was lie.

He thought she was about to say she didn't want to answer that question, but then, with the sky outside starting to lighten, she did.

'I'm the one who caused the hurt. I broke up my parents' marriage.'

He waited rather than respond.

'My father was head of music at my school.'

'High school?' he checked. 'Or do you call it senior school?'

'Senior.' She nodded. 'At the end of my first year there was some gossip about him and another teacher. I just ignored it. But after the summer the rumours got worse. My mother kept asking me what was wrong. She was worried, I guess. I was in my room, crying a lot, trying to hide it. She insisted I tell her. She said that she loved me, that she was concerned, and that I could tell her anything. So eventually I did.' She shrugged. 'She's never forgiven me for it.'

'And your father?'

'He's never forgiven me either. They don't say it, but I know they blame me.'

'For what?'

'The divorce...the change in circumstances. I'm quite sure they both wish I'd just shut the hell up. Anyway, they both married again and had new families.' She took a big breath. 'You don't need to hear all this.'

'I asked to hear it.'

'You did...' She looked pensive for a moment. 'Would you have said anything? If you'd found out your father was cheating?'

'I wouldn't have had to, the way people talk here. My mother would've known about it before he made it home.' Then he thought for a moment. 'I don't know,' he admitted.

She closed her eyes in relief at his honest answer—relief that he hadn't just dashed in and said she'd been right. Instead, he seemed to be considering it—and then he told her something about himself.

'I've never really shared what's on my mind. Dante was always the more emotional one.' He laughed. 'At my *nonna*'s funeral he asked me when she was coming back. I said she was dead, and he said, "I know that, but when is she coming back...?" So I told him—never. I got told off for upsetting him.'

He was quiet then, as if he was really considering her question. She could almost feel him thinking.

'No, I don't think I would have told my mother,' he said at last. 'But that's more a reflection on me...' He squeezed her arm. 'I would hate it, though, if you were mine...to think of you in bed crying and unable to come to me.'

'My mother said I could tell her anything. And then, when I did, she took her love away. And you're right—it hurt.' She nodded. 'Everything was taken away. Truly, I wish I'd never found out. Certainly I wish I'd never said anything.'

'You got through it, though.'

'Maybe...'

'Of course you did. You're here, aren't you...?'

Sex was their reward for sharing, and soon they lost themselves in each other.

She missed breakfast in the restaurant and it was inching past her check-out time as they lay there, breathless.

'I should go,' Juliet said. 'I have to check out.'

'Have a shower,' he suggested. 'I'll get your stuff brought up here so you don't have to rush off.'

She didn't want to rush off.

She liked it here an awful lot.

Sex had always seemed to her like a hurdle to be jumped over. She'd never thought of *after*. She rather wished it had been awful and awkward... Not really, but it might be easier to leave if it hadn't been so wonderful.

If *he* hadn't been so wonderful.

'You okay?' he checked.

'Perfect.'

'No regrets?'

'None.' She shook her head, and her smile stayed in

place, but she had to force it just a little, and there was a slight amendment taking place in her head.

She would deal with that later.

She dashed to his bathroom and bypassed the petals still strewn in the bath. She jumped in the shower, trying not to examine the thought that had occurred to her. After all, how could you possibly regret enjoying a lover too much? How could you regret your first time being so wonderful?

She found a new toothbrush in the little basket of goodies, and a bamboo comb, but her eyes lingered on his silver comb and heavy razor. She reached out for a heavy glass bottle, removing the stopper and almost folding at the delicious hit of his cologne. She breathed in the peppery, woody scent she'd first met in the lobby, and then later, so intimately, with her face in his neck, on his chest…

Don't think of that now.

She went to replace the stopper, but then ran it across her wrist. She'd think of him later, Juliet decided. Breathe him in when she was alone. Then she stared at herself and saw that her lips were plump from the attention. She also saw the slight panic flaring in her green eyes at the prospect of nonchalantly saying goodbye.

One night, she reminded herself, dabbing the stopper on her neck and somehow calming down, telling herself it was just as well their time was limited.

He could become very easy to fall for.

And far too hard to let go.

She wrapped herself in a towel and headed out, ready to put on last night's clothes. But all her things had been brought up from her room—her violin, even her flowers.

She went through her overnight bag and found the cheesecloth dress she'd arrived in—not that he'd seen it.

'The real me,' she said, snapping on her regular bra and smiling as he pulled a sulky face. Then she put on her dress and combed her hair, before sitting on the bed where he lay and pulling on her espadrilles.

'Do you want to do something today?'

Her hand paused for a second, then resumed tying the straps as she answered, 'I don't know...' She looked over as she carried on fastening her footwear.

'I could sort out your boss...'

'It would take more than charm.'

She was tense at the prospect of saying goodbye...tense at the thought of returning to Anna's.

Just tense.

He looked at her as she stood and walked over to the long mirror and leant forward, coiling her long red hair and tying it on top of her head in one practised movement.

The dress was the colour of sea glass and it brought out the red of her hair, and he watched as she did up a couple of buttons at the front.

'You could maybe try and talk to Anna...'

She didn't realise he was watching her, and he saw her roll her eyes a little, as if to ask what the hell he would know.

'I saw that.'

She caught his eye and the tension left her and she actually smiled—but she was clearly still certain he couldn't help.

'You don't play an instrument.'

'True.'

'And am I right in assuming it's not a house-share set-up at your place in Dubai, Sevandro?' she asked, with a twist of light sarcasm.

'I don't share my space with anyone.' His response was equally dry. 'I have a penthouse apartment looking out over the Persian Gulf.'

For a brief second he saw her there, pale on his coffee-coloured silk sheets, the glittering ocean behind her.

'But it's all soundproofed. I could have an entire orchestra playing and no one would hear a thing.'

'Exactly. And we don't all have PAs to arrange our schedules.'

She was smiling and teasing him through the mirror. And he'd been right, Sev decided. She wasn't shy—just nervous about reaching out. But once that contact had been made it was like watching a flower open.

'Do you want to go to the beach?' he offered.

'The beach? I don't have anything to swim in.'

'We can get something there. There are some nice boutiques. Besides, I still haven't wined and dined you, and nor have we danced. How about a little intense romance?'

'Like you used to know?' She laughed, but then it faded. 'When do you leave?'

It was perhaps an odd question, but she needed to know—needed a timeline to give to her heart.

'When do you go back to Dubai?'

'Tomorrow. Leave your things here, then I can drop you back at Anna's later tonight.'

That sounded doable, she told herself. And she wasn't going to fall any further in a day.

Except she looked to where he lay and felt as if he were beckoning her towards a slightly more perilous path. But she discounted the silent alert, glancing at the rumpled sheets where he lay, in the bed he'd taken her in.

'I'd love to go to the beach.'

CHAPTER FIVE

THERE WAS NOTHING WORSE, Juliet decided, than choosing a bikini in a high-end boutique. Especially when you had big breasts, a tiny assistant, and the sexiest man alive kept making dreadful suggestions.

'What about this one?'

'I'm too pale to wear white.'

She shunned his suggestion and grabbed a nice navy-blue—but 'safe' was not always 'nice'.

'The sun will soon be setting on our romantic day,' he warned from the other side of the curtain as she stood in the changing room, hating it. 'Let me see.'

She peeled back the curtain and there he stood—in what looked like black boxers, really, only ones for swimming. And of course with that body he was beach-ready.

He glanced over. 'I still think the white one.'

She put it on once more, to prove a point, sure she'd look like a milk bottle. But instead… The white was so white it brought out the scrap of colour in her skin.

'I'll get this one,' she said, about to close the curtain to take it off.

'Just put your dress on over it.'

He came over and dealt with the exclusive label that

hung from the top, his fingers light on the side of her ribs. It felt as deep as a thorough kiss.

'And this one,' he said, flicking out the label on the bikini bottom, the heat of his hand on the small of her back.

'Will we…?' She closed her eyes, stopping herself from asking if they might skip the beach and go directly to bed—not because she didn't want the bed, but because she wanted this day too. 'I might need sunblock.'

They walked out, she with her boring underwear in her bag, and then he told her he was getting factor one million sunblock for her and to wait there.

Juliet would have liked a moment to examine last night, to just go over all the bliss, but there would be many days and nights for that, so she wandered off and then stared into a window at a cream dress that would, if it were black, be the perfect concert dress. It was utterly gorgeous…

'Why are you gazing at a wedding dress as if you have to have it *now*?' His hand came to her shoulder. 'That's not intense, Juliet. That's scary…'

'I didn't know…' She laughed and looked up, and sure enough it was a bridal boutique. 'That's my perfect concert dress. Well, apart from the colour. And the scoop neck is a bit low.'

'Try it on.'

'No.

'Go on…' he insisted.

'No. Because you'll buy it for me, like you bought the bikini, and—'

'Juliet.' He cut that thought off at the neck before it had even formed. 'I told you I don't buy gifts. The bikini was necessary. And believe me, I am not buying you a dress from a bridal shop—just try it on.'

He made the impossible easier, by just walking in, and then she had to take off her new bikini top, and then the assistant told her the 'perfect dress' was actually not only too small, but not even a complete dress.

'This is just a base,' she explained to Sevandro, almost apologetically. 'We were about to dress the window…'

'No…' Juliet shook her head. 'It's gorgeous as it is.' She gazed into the mirror. It was very plain, and that was what she liked. 'Well, it is a little low…' She looked over to Sev. 'And the sleeves…' She explained all the factors she had to take into consideration for a concert dress. 'I'd have to have three-quarter sleeves, and the shoulders are a bit…' She ran a hand over the seams and tried to decide on a word. 'Pointy.'

'Pointy?' The assistant's lips pulled just a fraction. She was clearly thinking her a little diva, and not really understanding that she was discussing her requirements for work.

They had gelato for a very late breakfast, in a cone as they walked to the promenade.

'You should get something specially made,' he told her.

'I'm saving for a violin first,' she explained, as they stepped onto the golden beach and walked to the very nice loungers. 'Well, it's the one I play, but I'm renting it at the moment.'

'Just get a dress!' He looked at her. 'I'd be terrible at being poor…'

He was so bad he was good, and he made her laugh rather than feel embarrassed to strip down to her bikini on a gorgeous beach, and he slathered her in so much sun cream, and moved the umbrellas to the nth degree.

She felt…

Protected.

Factor fifty plus, plus, plus.

For the first time since she was twelve years old and it had all fallen away she felt looked after.

'It's beautiful here.' She rolled onto her stomach and looked at the gorgeous resort behind them. 'But I think this is a private beach...'

'It is.' He yawned. 'I used to work here. And then I bought it.'

'Is this where you...?' She put out a leg and lightly kicked him. 'Your first lover?'

'No,' he said. 'That hotel's a little further along the promenade. But this is the first hotel I owned, or at least part-owned, with Sheikh Mahir.'

'Wow...' She blinked. 'What's he like?'

'He's okay.' He put his arm up over his head, his eyes closed against the morning sun. 'We argue, but for the most part we get on.'

'What do you argue about?'

He smiled and gave a soft half-laugh, because he'd never really discussed it or pondered it. These were not the sort of questions his family or anyone really asked.

And even if they did?

He wasn't sure he'd answer.

The regular rules didn't seem to apply today. It was as if he and Juliet had a different operating manual—an access-all-areas code. Even if some of those areas perhaps weren't that interesting...

'Mahir likes to think his son, Adal, works harder than he does. I went to school with him. He hasn't changed at all.'

'Do you get on with Adal?'

'Not lately. This latest project—the new hotel—there

isn't the scope to carry someone or pretend that the golden son is pulling his weight.'

'You've told them that?'

'Yes.' He breathed out heavily and then closed his eyes, surprised to have shared as much.

'And?' she asked.

He smiled at her curiosity and her impatience to know the result.

'They're still sulking.'

It was nice to just lie together and enjoy the sound of the ocean and occasional conversation. To just lie there and let her eyes drift over him.

His body was magnificent, and she stuck out a leg and held it near his.

'I'm so pale...'

Especially next to his skin, which seemed to soak in the Mediterranean sun and darken in the bright light.

Then her calf dusted his lower thigh and he caught her leg and held it there. And then they were not thinking of skin.

They ventured into the water, and it was a little cooler than his skin and whole lot warmer than she'd braced herself for.

'Do you go to the beach in Dubai?' she asked as they waded out.

'No.'

'Do you go in the pool?'

'No.' He shook his head, pulled her into him. 'I do have a yacht. It's all for work, though.'

He crossed his eyes and made her laugh.

'If I want people to pay for, design, build and furnish my beautiful hotel, I have to chat them up.'

He kissed her then, as he would have liked to on the beach, right there in the water. He tasted her sunblock and didn't care. His tongue was coaxing hers to tangle with his, to move in his mouth and suggest all the things they wanted to do.

'We should get you into the shade,' he said, his hands holding her waist as she sizzled beneath him. 'You are very red.'

It wasn't from the sun.

And they remained in the sea, jumping small waves and messing about as he told her about the Dubai skyline, and the incredible night-life.

'It's not all clubs and bars—there is a beautiful classical music scene. It's an exciting country, full of ambition—you'd love it.'

'I don't know,' she said as they lay back in the water. 'I love Lucca.'

They lay on their backs and floated like otters. He reached for her hand and held on and she knew this was just fleeting, and possibly he was just the best flirt, good at making her feel relaxed and nice, but she loved his charming ways and how, as they drifted, still they spoke.

'How long will you be here?' he asked.

'For good, I hope,' she said, squinting at the high sun. 'I'll apply for residency in a couple of years, so long as work is going okay. I hope things are going well by then. I'll have the quartet, maybe a chair in an orchestra or regular substitute work.' She laughed at herself. 'I'll give you a discreet wave if I see you on the walls with some gorgeous date.'

'You won't see me,' Sev said, and then his voice was serious. 'This goes no further...?'

'Of course.'

'Once the memorial service is out of the way I'm not coming back here.'

The warm sea suddenly felt like ice, and she knew what she was being told was serious indeed.

'I have a property here, which I'm putting on the market, and there are a couple of things I'd hoped to sort...' He didn't elaborate. 'That may not be possible now, but I want things in the best order they can be.'

He had a plan.

Sevandro really was preparing to leave.

'For good?' she checked, and stood up in the water. 'What about Gio?'

'Of course I'll come if there's an emergency, but no more family events, or Christmases, or the million and one other reasons to return.'

'What about...?' she started, then shook her head.

They were sharing what they chose to and not probing. They were close because both knew that this connection was something short-lived and fragile, something both would respect.

'Do Dante and Susie know?'

'I think they have an idea.'

She thought about that pause yesterday, during his speech, how his smile had faded when she'd mentioned the christening. It hadn't been the mention of double dates that had caused that reaction.

They went back to the beach and dried off as her mind caught up with all that he'd said, all that she'd seen.

'You're not coming back to see the baby?'

'No.'

She didn't like that answer. She didn't like his cold decision. But his future wasn't her business. This wasn't about agreeing with each other, it was about being there for each other for a little while.

'They can visit me in Dubai if they want to.'

He was almost the scowling man she'd first seen, she thought.

'Dante doesn't want us to be close.'

'What about Gio and Mimi?'

'We can meet in Rome.' He pulled on his linen shirt. 'Gio will hopefully live another twenty years, but I can't keep coming back.' He looked over. 'Same as yours...' he said. 'Not all families work.'

And soon the most wonderful day—apart from that bit—ended with seafood and limoncello spritzers for her, still water for him, and sexy music pulsing from a dancefloor.

And as they danced to the pulsing beat she kept waiting for a hotel to appear, or a bed—something to blot out what he'd said.

He was never coming back.

Oh, make that maybe once.

This really was all they'd have.

It was a winding drive home, and Juliet felt her eyes grow heavy.

'Sleep,' he told her.

'No, it's rude.'

Not only that—she didn't want to miss a moment.

'We haven't sorted out your boss...' he said.

'I'll sort her...' She gave a weary sigh. 'I'm going to get up earlier each day to fit the chores in, and I'll use the rooms at school for practice.'

'Aren't you already doing that?'

'Yes,' she agreed, leaning her head on the window, wishing they could turn the car around and go back. 'But once my exams are done...'

She didn't finish her sentence, and as she dozed Sev glanced over a couple of times, seeing her there, sandy and her limbs pink, as the streetlights flashed.

Thinking.

About leaving.

About coming home for the last time.

About her.

They passed through Casadio land—row after row of vines. Some planted when his parents had been born...others when he and Dante had.

They passed the entrance to the winery...passed Villa Casadio, where Christos lived.

Then they passed the De Santis winery, where Rosa's family still lived, and again he glanced over to where Juliet slept.

Her legs were stretched out, her head in an awkward position, and he reached out an arm and moved her a little, then reclined her seat. He let her sleep, resisting the urge to wake her, to tell her about his doubts about Rosa's pregnancy that lived only in his head.

He drove past the church where they'd married...where Rosa now lay.

Where he'd sworn on her grave never to share his doubts with another person. To let her rest, lie in peace...

There was no peace for him, though.

* * *

She felt the motion of the car change, or perhaps there were lights, or the sound of the indicator blinking, but she knew the end of their time was here.

Her subconscious tried to be kind and pull her back to sleep.

She never wanted this day to end.

'Juliet?'

She stirred and gave a nod. She knew they were at Anna's, and knew she had to somehow brace herself for goodbye.

'Come on.'

She was still half asleep and not wanting to wake up as he offered his hand and she stepped out of the car.

'I was really asleep!' She laughed, leaning on him more than she ever had so far. She frowned. 'We need to get my things from the hotel…' She was fuzzy from too much sun and too little sleep and the company of Sevandro. 'Wait—this isn't Anna's…'

This definitely wasn't Anna's. There were some gates that he opened, and then he took her hand and led her through a neglected garden and up some stone stairs.

Even neglected it was way beyond Anna's garden…

Sevandro…or was it Sev—she still hadn't made up her mind which name she preferred—was pressing a code into the panel next to a large front door. The lock clicked and he pushed the heavy door open and led her inside.

'Where are we?' Juliet asked as he flicked a switch and a beautiful and very large hall came into the light.

'Welcome to Mars.'

CHAPTER SIX

'OH, MY…'

The house was stunning.

Cold and empty, yet beautiful indeed, its floors were marble and the ceilings high, and she could have happily lingered just in the hall. But she followed him and found herself in a vast room—again empty, except for an elegant chandelier that he turned on and dimmed. Little beams of light danced around the vacant space and she walked to the massive fireplace, where the mantelpiece was higher than herself.

'It's going on the market,' Sevandro explained.

'It's yours?'

He nodded.

'But why stay in hotels if you have this?' She winced. 'Or was this where you and Rosa lived?'

'No.' He shook his head. 'Rosa took one look and hated it—we never spent a single night here. She wanted Villa Casadio.'

'Where's that?'

He didn't answer straight away, just walked on, and although she would have loved to linger she followed him out, gazed into room after empty room.

* * *

'Look at this library!'

Juliet's enthusiasm, even at three in the morning, with the place cold and bare, was a stark contrast to Rosa's reaction. Though it wasn't Rosa's view he was comparing it to—it was his. The first time he'd seen the property he'd been composed and impassive with the realtor, but inside he had felt as Juliet now did.

She wasn't following him around any more. She was exploring back in the main hall, standing at the bottom of the spiral staircase gazing up, her mouth open.

'If we go down one level…' he started,

But Juliet was already making her way up.

She paused. 'Can I?'

'Of course.'

'Sevandro, it is beautiful.'

She peered into a bathroom, tried to turn on the light, but had to rely on the moon shining in through frosted windows onto huge mirrors illuminating a central clawfoot bath.

'Oh, my…'

'I had a domestic team come in last week to get it ready to go on the market. There's still more to do. A *lot* more to do,' he added. 'Still, it's probably better than I remember it.'

Far better—he hadn't set foot in the place since he'd come to visit Gio at Christmas, and even then it had been a cursory look around, as he'd decided to put it on the market. It had been freezing then, neglected and dusty, but he rather thought she would have loved it even so.

'The realtor suggests I get a few rooms styled.'

'Why? Anyone can see it's gorgeous. But you need a piano in the lounge…' She gave him her opinion. 'And navy silk couches.'

'Maybe… The main bedroom has all the original fur-nishings. I like it, but the realtor said it's a disaster.'

He attempted to turn on the lights there, but again they didn't work.

It didn't matter.

'It's beautiful.' She walked around the large shadowy space, touching a chaise and then walking over to the vel-vety bed. 'Why would the realtor call it a disaster?'

'I think it's a love or hate thing. It's red,' he told her. 'Very red. The carpets, the bedding, the walls. And when the drapes are hung, they are red too.' He watched her sit-ting on the bed and walked over. 'So, what do you say?'

'What do I say? That it's stunning and that I cannot be-lieve you stay in hotels rather than here. And that this…' she sank back '…is the best bed ever.'

She wasn't even flirting. She was so tired, and the sleep in the car had served only to remind her how exhausted she was.

'I don't know what else to say. I love it.'

'I meant what do you say about staying here?'

In the shadowy light he saw her immediate frown, and it surprised him that it hadn't entered her head why he had brought her here. Her reaction to his home was pure, he knew.

'Living here for a while?' he went on.

'In your home?'

'It's never been my home. And don't worry—I'm not asking you to move in with me.' He laughed at the no-tion. 'But you do need some space, and these are important months for you. I won't be here—it's going to be empty. Maybe you could just come here to practise?'

It was tempting…so tempting. But it was just too generous.

As well, there was a deeper truth: she was developing more than a crush on him. It scared her how much she liked him. A man who was about to turn his back on his family… a man who was close to no one.

'I don't think so.'

He lay down too, and they stared up at the ceiling, then wriggled and got comfortable, just lay side by side.

'No, it's too…'

'What?'

'Too much.'

'It's just sitting here empty. You can tell Susie and Dante that we spoke at the wedding…that I need someone to open up and such while tradesmen come through.' He shrugged. 'I probably do need someone.'

'What about when you're here?'

'I shan't be here. I'll try to fly in and out for the memorial, but I'm not even sure I'll have time for that. The pace at work is crazy—and that's before we've even signed off on the project. After that, it will be worse.'

'Why, though?' She stared. 'We agreed on one night only.'

'We did. You don't have time for a relationship and I don't want one. But it is good talking to you. Having…' He hesitated, as if he didn't know what to call it. 'This.'

'Yes…'

'I'm not just selling the house,' he admitted. 'I have some loose ends to tie up—things I need to sort out. Hopefully

I can clear the air with Dante…leave things the best I can. Who knows? They might come and see me in Dubai.'

'What sort of things?'

'You know that Dante and I fought?'

She nodded.

'Dante asked if Rosa was pregnant—insinuating it was a trap, a grab for our land—there's lots of history between our two wineries. I didn't want to hear it.'

'Of course not.'

'I told him he was wrong.' He turned and looked at her then. 'However, that wasn't true. Rosa had indeed told me she was having my baby…'

'That's why you married?

'Yes.'

'Had you been together for long?'

'We never dated,' he said. 'It was just one night. I had just found out I'd got the loan from Mahir… I was supposed to be celebrating with my family.' He turned and stared up at the ceiling now rather than at her. 'I'm sure you don't want the details.'

'I do.'

It was an odd admission, yet lying here in the semi-darkness, at the end of such a glorious night and day, she somehow knew this was the only chance she'd get to hear them. It was like collecting tiny pearls scattered on the floor, each one a treasure, and she wanted all the precious pearls.

'If you want to tell me, of course.'

'I went to the De Santis winery. I thought we were meeting there—I'm not sure if the message was relayed wrong. Anyway, Rosa came over. She'd seen my car arrive, and she didn't know what I was celebrating.' He shrugged. 'Things just happened…'

Juliet swallowed. She understood how.

'That night I was careless, and when she told me she was pregnant, that her mother had already worked it out, there was no question I'd do the right thing.'

'No question?' she checked.

'Some questions,' he admitted in the still pre-dawn. 'But I kept them to myself.' He looked over. 'I'd never expected to marry.'

'Why?'

'I don't know,' he admitted. 'It just wasn't something I could envisage. You?' he asked, perhaps needing a break from his own thoughts.

'I used to want to…' she nodded. 'When I was younger. But then…' She paused. 'I think my father's affair messed me up.'

'Or your mother turning off her love like a tap when she didn't like what you had to say.'

His summing up was cold, even a bit brutal, but possibly it was required, because it cleared the mists around that time a fraction.

'Maybe.' She actually smiled. 'You can be very direct.'

'I know.' He half laughed. 'So can my brother. The night before I got married, when he tried to suggest it was a trap, I didn't appreciate it. I think most people had guessed it was a shotgun marriage, but I wasn't going to confirm it. It didn't seem like the best start for us, and I didn't want our child knowing we'd only married for their sake.' He took a breath. 'So I told him to go to hell and we fought.'

She nodded.

'Rosa lost the baby just after the wedding. At least that's what she told me.'

Juliet frowned. 'I don't know what you mean…'

'I think I got so angry with Dante because I was already starting to have doubts that she was pregnant myself.'

'You think she lied?'

'I do. But I don't know for sure. I was about to go looking for answers when the accident happened.'

Was this the *'more'* that Susie had been unable to talk about? Juliet wondered.

'Does Dante know any of this?'

'No. After her funeral he apologised—said he'd clearly got it wrong...'

'You never told your family she was expecting?'

'No. Rosa didn't want anyone apart from her parents to know she was pregnant until well after the wedding. After the miscarriage she said we could try again.' He gave a mirthless laugh. 'Even though we'd never tried in the first place.'

Juliet sat up on the bed, really thinking about all he'd said. 'So they all think you married for love?'

'They do,' he agreed. 'I've never wanted to fall in love and marry. I didn't then, and certainly not now. But when I messed up I knew I had to do the right thing. On a selfish level, having a wife and baby suited my career. Sheikh Mahir is very family orientated. We're partners now, but I was new to him then. He was very pleased I was settling down.'

'Were you upset when Rosa told you she'd lost the baby?'

He looked at her for the longest moment, and then nodded. When she heard him swallow, Juliet guessed why he didn't speak.

'I'm sorry.' She blew out a breath. 'I get it now,' she told him. 'I get why you hate coming back to Lucca. Can you talk to Dante? Tell him he was right?'

'I still don't know for sure, though, and it seems unfair

on Rosa to speculate when she isn't here to state her case. I was thinking of speaking to her doctor. He stitched me and Dante up that night of the fight, and he said a couple of things that have always stayed with me.'

'Such as…?'

'My hand was swollen and he said, "Your bride isn't going to be pleased if you can't put your ring on." Then he asked how Rosa was. I didn't think anything of it at the time, but when I look back he was asking as if he hadn't seen her for a while.'

'What else?'

'It was small things… He asked if I had any questions for him. I thought he was talking about my hand. But maybe he was inviting me to speak about something else?'

'Could you try asking him now?'

'It's too late. I spoke to his daughter at the wedding reception—not about this, but I asked after him. She told me he has dementia, so that window is now closed.' He shrugged. 'Don't worry about it.' He pulled her close. 'Forget about it now.'

He wanted to get back to the way they'd been, and so too did Juliet—she didn't want them to end on this low. But what he'd told her was important.

'I think I'd tell Dante,' she said.

'Well, you would say that, wouldn't you?'

Was he referring to her telling her mother about her father's affair? Surely not.

'But look at the trouble telling tales got you into last time.'

He was!

'Sevandro!' She was jolted—utterly shocked. 'You can't say that!'

But he had. And she was so shocked that she laughed. And the fact that he *could* joke, and she *could* laugh about something so dreadful, was a revelation in itself,

'*Spiona!*' he called her.

That meant tattletale. They had a sort of wrestle as he said it, and it was the most inappropriate fun she had ever had. And as they play-fought it was as if she was banishing the sting of that day, making a new memory of it that would always make her laugh.

She ended up on his stomach, legs astride him, and she knew there wasn't another person on this planet who could have teased her like that, who could have taken the most painful dark part of her and soothed it.

'So,' he said, with a smile that melted her. 'Are you going to be my housekeeper?'

Was she?

'No strings,' he told her. 'You know. I don't do all that.'

'I know.' She said, and then paused. 'Strings are my speciality, though.'

He gave a half-laugh at her reference to her violin, but she saw that he didn't get what she was trying to say. Juliet didn't know how to say it, but knew she had to try. She was exploring the boundaries of her own heart as she looked at the only man she'd ever been with…the only man she'd ever wanted to be with. But there were conditions.

'I can't be your lover in Lucca.'

'I'm not asking you to be a kept woman.'

'I understand that.'

'If I come back for the memorial I'll stay in a hotel—no problem.' He gave her a smile. 'Unless you want me?'

His hands slid up her outer thighs, warm and firm, then back down, and then they moved over the soft, sensitive skin of her inner thighs and she saw the arrogance in his smile.

He knew there was no question she would want him.

'Sev.' She put her hand over his, stopped his sensual stealth and looked right into his eyes. 'If you leave now and meet someone tomorrow, that's fine.' She swallowed, because that wasn't quite true. 'It might hurt, but that's fine. We shan't have this again.' She removed his hand from her thigh.

'I don't know what you mean.'

'If you come back for the memorial and there's been someone else…' She shook her head.

'Hold on… You want us to act like a couple, yet we'll be continents apart and not see each other for months—not see anyone—all because of one night?' He laughed at the ridiculousness of it, pulling back his hands of his own accord, clearly not used to such demands. 'I told you: I don't do relationships.'

'I'm just letting you know. And if I do stay here, and I meet someone, I'll move out.'

He frowned.

'I assume you won't want me bringing men back here?'

She watched his lips tighten, and his eyes darkened as they met hers. Possibly he'd got where she was coming from.

'They're two separate issues.'

He was sulking, and he looked so sexy, but then he gave a small smile, undoing the buttons on her dress, untying the strings of the bikini beneath.

Toying with her naked breasts, he came up with a possible solution. 'You could come to Dubai now and then…'

He moved up onto his elbows and blew on a nipple.

'I don't have time,' she pointed out, closing her eyes as his mouth took it in, feeling weak, and yet certain, alight with so many different responses to him. 'You know that.'

'We'll have to make time.' He came up from her wet breast and looked at her. 'Look, I really can't come back here. And I'm not talking about family now. Work is about to kick off…'

But then perhaps he remembered her exams, and the reasons she needed to retreat from the world, because he cursed and lay back down.

'I don't *do* the couple thing.'

He was seriously pissed off.

'I'm not demanding anything, Sev,' Juliet told him. 'Just letting you know.'

He lay silent and she sat up, her thighs warm from their day on the beach, loose against his loins. They were both firmly in their corners, but united in their turn-on.

'Okay…' he half relented. 'I shan't lay a finger on you again if there's been anyone else.'

'Excellent,' she said. 'And if I meet anyone—'

'Please…' He gave a low laugh as his hand returned, pulling at the ties of her bikini bottom this time, playing with the titian curls there, then slipping his hand down and feeling her oiled and warm. 'I don't think there'll be an issue there.'

Oh, she wanted to give a smart reply—to tell him not to be so certain. Yet she knew it would be pointless, and she knew, even if they ended things today, it would take a lot of time to get over him.

She also knew, even as he stroked inside her, even as he withdrew his fingers and gave his attention to the swollen knot of nerves there, that she was much too into him.

'Nice?' he asked needlessly, as she moaned, and he told her with his hand that no one could ever please her the way he did.

'I want…'

Her thighs were shaking, and she gave a frustrated sob as he ceased in his attention, left her on the edge. And there she remained, hovering for a moment, as he unbelted himself, then tugged at the buttons on his shirt, exposing his chest as he rolled on a condom.

'What do you want?' he asked, guiding her on to him.

'This,' she said, trying to focus simply on the sheer pleasure their bodies made, moving on him.

He pulled her head down and they were kissing, her breasts flattening on his chest and his hands moving her, her cheek beside his.

'Move in…' he said, his voice husky, his fingers digging into her hips and grinding her down on him. 'There'll be more of this.'

She nodded, perhaps unseen, but it was as if she was re-assuring herself. There would be more of this…

The want, the desire, was all new to her, so deep and acute, and even before he was gone she was missing him already.

'Don't cry.'

She heard his words and knew that she must be crying.

'Cry, then,' he said. 'It's been tough for you.'

His voice was ragged. Perhaps he thought she was simply relieved that her housing and financial woes were gone.

She was crying for other reasons, though. For making love while trying not to lose her heart…

He was stroking her bottom, and she realised she was moving now of her own accord. Or were they both moving as one? There were strings, invisible threads lacing them, pulling her closer, opening her up, tightening her centre.

The sound he made as he released was a perfect note—*her* perfect note—and it had her tightening and pulsing as he shot inside.

Her face was on his cheek as she drew in a breath, waiting to come back down to earth.

Normality should be pinging in now, Juliet thought.

'I'm going to miss you,' he told her.

And she felt her lips pinch on tears as she wondered why he got to say it while she dared not.

It was starting to get light, and they both knew they had to get her things from the hotel.

As they rearranged their clothes he spoke.

'Take some time. Think it through before you tell Anna you're leaving.'

'I've already said yes.'

'Never believe or be held to what's said during sex,' he told her. 'Think about what you really want.'

He was businesslike now, as he wrote down the entrance code.

'I'll need your phone number.'

They went through a few things as daylight started to filter in and the room was tinged red, then they headed down the stairs.

'Listen, if it sells quickly, I won't hand it over till your exams are done. Is that fair?' he asked.

'More than fair.'

She watched him look around, perhaps realising that it might sell fast and that possibly he might never see the place again. She felt a flutter of panic—because he really was closing things down here.

'When do you fly?' she asked at the hotel, as her things were loaded into the car.

'Midday. I'll have breakfast with Mimi and Gio. Do you think I can get them to come and see me in Dubai?'

'Good luck with that!' She laughed.

He drove her to Anna's and it was still only six a.m. as he pulled up.

'This was great,' Sevandro said. 'I didn't expect to have such a nice weekend. You?'

'I hoped to,' she admitted. 'Though it did exceed all expectations.'

They shared a smile—their smile, the one that repeated their words back to each other—but no kiss.

'We'll keep it between us?' she checked. 'Especially with me moving in?'

'Sure. Anyway, I'll be in Dubai.'

'Yes.'

'But I'll hopefully see you after the memorial,' he said, because three months of abstinence was rather a big commitment for him to make.

And she got that.

'I'll hopefully see you, too.'

She felt like a different person as she walked up the driveway to Anna's. Dawn was breaking and little birds were chirping. She turned to wave, or rather to hold up her violin, but he had already gone.

Get used to that feeling, Juliet told herself. *One day soon Sevandro will be gone for ever.*

CHAPTER SEVEN

MARS WAS GORGEOUS at this time of year!

Or at least the version of Mars Sev had given her.

Anna hadn't been best pleased when Juliet had told her she was leaving, but soon she had begun moving her things and was now installed in the beautiful home.

In the week it had taken to work her notice, Sevandro had arranged for a lot to be done.

The dust sheets had gone, the windows had all been cleaned, drapes had been hung and there was a large grey velvet couch in the lounge, with a few occasional tables. The lights all worked now, and there were towels and new linen.

The room she loved the most, though, was the main bedroom.

It was incredible.

It wasn't just red, as Sevandro had described, but a blushing crimson—from the walls to the carpets, from the drapes to the bedding—with just the occasional splash of gold around the mirrors and on handles and such.

'How is it?'

He called her on the very first night she was there—although perhaps that was to check on things at the house, rather than to check on her.

'Gorgeous…' She sighed. 'Peaceful! I can't believe I'm in the middle of Lucca—I feel like I'm out in the country.'

She looked around the crimson bedroom, examining it again now she'd turned on the side lights. It was the most sensual room on earth—like a womb or something. All red, even this huge plump bed, also dressed in crimson.

'It should be too much.'

'What should?'

'The flagrant use of crimson.'

'Is that how to tell me you're in my bed, without telling me you're in my bed?' he grumbled.

But she laughed. 'It's my favourite room,' she told him.

And not just because it was beautiful. Because it was the room where they'd made love, where she'd cried as she came to him. The room where they'd spoken so intimately…

Her music flourished, and at the end of each day she filled her schedule with little triumphant ticks, but it worried her that a day only truly became a gold star one when Sevandro called.

More often than not it was Helene, his PA, who called to inform her of tradesmen arriving, or photographers, or gardeners and so on. But every now and then there was the bliss of his voice for a few moments—a giddy high, followed by the comedown of silence when he rang off. And then a few moments when she sat quietly acknowledging the rapid beat of her own heart at the mere sound of his voice, the lift it gave her night or day.

It unsettled her.

Even if she hadn't made all the right choices, and it felt lonely at times, Juliet was used to relying only on herself and providing for herself. It wasn't so much the fact that she was staying in his property that unnerved her—she knew it was temporary, and was simply grateful for the chance to give her all to her music in these important months—it was her deepening feelings for Sevandro that unsettled her.

She could ignore her feelings as she wrestled with her exam pieces or attended rehearsals and caught up with friends. But at the end of their brief phone calls, or at night when she fell into bed, there were moments of silence where she did her best to ignore what her heart was telling her.

You like him too much.

Of course she did, Juliet would reason. She wouldn't have slept with him otherwise.

You're in too deep.

No. Thank you, heart, for the unnecessary warning, but I know what I'm doing...

Susie and Dante returned, and they had a quick catch-up, but Susie was busy juggling her new apprenticeship at Pearla's, and Dante being half in Milan and half in Lucca, as well as being pregnant.

But she brought lunch over to Juliet one day, and they sat on the portico looking out on the garden that was starting to take shape as the gardeners cut back the overgrowth.

'Wow,' Susie said, 'when did that fountain appear?'

'Last week.' Juliet smiled. 'Tomorrow they're filling the swimming pool.'

Susie completely believed that she and Sev had simply come to an arrangement about the house. The thought of her and Sev in a relationship of any sort had obviously been instantly dismissed. It was clearly easier to believe she was just the temporary housekeeper.

'Does it disturb your practice?' Susie asked. 'All these workmen?'

'No.' Juliet shook her head. 'And it's nice knowing they don't care about my noise. There's a basement room if it gets too much—it looks like it was a dance studio. I take myself down there sometimes, but for the most part…'

For the most part life was perfect. All the problems she'd had were gone. But nature did indeed love a void, and now she had a whole new set of concerns.

'Sev has asked Gio and Mimi if they would consider Christmas in Dubai,' Susie told her. 'Dante doesn't think Sev's ever coming back.'

Juliet chewed on a fat strawberry and tried to think what she might have said if she and Sev hadn't shared so much— if she didn't know so much.

'Well, he'll be coming back here to see the baby.'

'I don't think so…' Susie sighed. 'He told Dante that he doesn't know if he'll even be able to get back for the memorial.'

'Surely…?'

Juliet halted herself in her delving and asking for more details, but surely Susie had it wrong. She tried to keep her question vague, and not reveal the panic at the thought of not even seeing him one final time.

'It's the ten-year memorial, isn't it?'

'Yes,' Susie confirmed. 'But he's busy with work, apparently. How cold is that?'

Juliet didn't ask Sev about it when they spoke—didn't ask him to confirm if he was coming home one last time.

Perhaps she was too scared of his answer and having to

face her feelings. It felt safer and certainly more sensible to focus on her music...to utilise this golden opportunity.

Occasionally she called him—usually regarding the house, or the garden. But on the eve of her first exam it was for a very personal reason that Juliet rang him, bracing herself to get his voicemail, unsure if she was right to interfere.

'Ready for your exam?' he asked.

'I hope so. What are you doing?'

'Looking at a gap in the skyline.'

'The one you and Sheikh Mahir are hoping to fill?'

He'd told her a little about the dazzling complex that he was aiming to get off the ground.

'It sounds incredible,' she said.

'I'll send you a picture.'

He did, and she stared at the beautiful Dubai skyline he gazed upon tonight.

'Did you get it?' he asked.

'Yes...'

He wanted to know what she thought—wanted to know if he should be thinking the way he was.

'What do you think?' he pressed.

'It's stunning,' she said. 'Are you outside now?'

'Yes—just having a drink on the balcony... We're hoping to sign off on it all soon.'

'How soon?'

'A few weeks...then life gets even busier.'

She guessed that meant no trips to Lucca—not even for the memorial. He was shifting his base to Dubai completely, and she felt teary all of a sudden, nervous about what she had to say.

'Sev, the reason I called… Look, I don't know if I should say anything…'

'Is Susie asking awkward questions?'

'No, she's delighted that I've got somewhere to stay and that your home's being taken care of.' She took a breath. 'I went to the doctor a couple of weeks ago.'

'You're okay?'

She heard the cautious note in his voice and it was merited, given what had happened with Rosa, and how careful they'd been.

'Absolutely fine,' she told him.

Should she tell him she'd gone on the Pill? That she ached for it to be the day of the memorial, a few weeks from now? That she so badly wanted it to be a day he actually dreaded?

How selfish was that?

'So, what are you telling me?' he asked.

'I think the doctor was the lady you were talking to at the wedding.'

'Ella?' he checked.

'I think so… Is she the daughter of the doctor you were telling me about?' She heard only silence. 'Could you maybe speak with her about Rosa?'

'She wasn't practising ten years ago.'

Juliet was flustered. 'I guess not… It was just a thought… maybe there are old notes?'

'Yes.'

He was still a bit terse, but Juliet knew he was thinking about what she'd said. The silence was a long one, and she wondered if she shouldn't have said anything, just let it go.

'I'll let you get back to your skyline,' she told him.

'Good luck tomorrow.'

* * *

Sevandro did get back to the skyline, but his thoughts were of home. Not so much of the past, but the present.

Telling Juliet about Rosa had changed things—she was the first person he'd opened up to...the first person to hear his doubts about the baby.

For a decade he'd thought it best to leave things alone, but her gentle enquiry today had matched his own thoughts, her call a quiet confirmation of what he'd felt on Dante's wedding night.

He needed to know.

And not just for himself.

He thought of the grief that came around each and every year—the hollow feeling when he didn't know if he was thinking of a child who'd be almost ten or a wife who'd lied. Rather than take to whisky, he always made sure he worked impossibly late as the date approached, and in the days after, burying himself in work rather than dealing with the past.

No more.

Sevandro didn't call to check how her exam had gone.

Nor did he call the next day.

Or the next.

Weeks were flying...summer was fading.

And of course it wasn't a romance—because there were no texts, few calls... In truth, there was nothing.

To celebrate her final exam she and Susie decided on a catch-up lunch at Pearla's. Such an extravagance would have been unthinkable a few short weeks ago, but things were going well. So well that for the first time in ages Juliet had bought new clothes that had nothing to do with work—a navy linen dress that buttoned up the front and was smart enough for auditions and lunch with a friend.

'Oh, it's so good to see you!' Susie hugged her.

'It's brilliant to be out,' Juliet admitted. 'It feels like I've been shut away.'

'You have been.'

'Susie!' Everyone in the kitchen seemed to cry out in unison as they entered. 'We miss you.'

'I miss you too,' she said. 'I'll come over for a chat in a minute.'

First, though, they took their seats.

'Have you finished up here?' Juliet checked, knowing that Susie had wanted to do a few more weeks at the restaurant before she went on maternity leave.

'I spoke to Cuoco yesterday and told him I have to stop.'

'Everything's okay?'

'Of course! We're just so busy, with Dante between here and Milan and the winery… I'll be back next year, once the baby's here.' She patted her very nice bump. 'How were the exams?'

'I think they went okay… Well, I know a couple of them went really well.'

'And rehearsals?'

'They start next week,' Juliet said, then crossed her fingers. 'I'm practising loads.'

'You'll be wonderful—we can't wait.'

It wasn't just that Juliet's accommodation was sorted and her exams were over. Bookings for the ensemble were picking up, the weeks and months ahead were starting to be filled in, and she was starting to believe that she might be able to support herself in the town she loved with her music.

They chatted about everything and nothing, and it was so lovely to catch up.

Juliet was adamant that they went halves. 'Susie, please,' she said. 'I am finally making headway, and I don't want you paying for everything when we're out.'

'I wouldn't have said Pearla's in that case.'

'Then I wouldn't have had the best truffle carbonara!' Juliet beamed. 'And you do get a staff discount!'

'True!'

'Now I have to dash. I need to pay the rent.'

'Sev's *charging* you?'

'No!' She laughed. 'For my violin.'

'He's out with Dante right now…'

'Sorry?' Juliet was sure she'd misheard.

'Sev's home. Well, he's in his usual hotel,' Susie said. 'He flew in yesterday, apparently, and asked Dante if they could catch up.'

'That's nice…'

Juliet didn't know what else to say, or even how she felt. Sev was here in Lucca and she didn't even know.

They said goodbye, but just before Susie went to talk to her colleagues she changed her mind. 'Oh, I forgot…'

'What?'

'Gio's decided to go all out for the memorial.'

'Oh.' She thought about how Sev was already dreading it, and then was startled as Susie spoke on.

'Can you guys play?'

'Us?'

'Of course. Gio won't hear of anyone else.'

She told her the date and Juliet didn't quite know what to say.

'Do you already have a booking?' asked Susie. 'Or…?'

'I'm not sure…' She honestly didn't know what to do. 'Let me check with Louanna—she deals with that side of things.'

Louanna would jump at the chance, and of course the prospect should be churning her up as she walked. But instead the fact that Sev was here in Lucca was her biggest issue now.

Sevandro was here and she hadn't even known.

She took out her phone—not to call him, but to see if there had been any attempt by him to contact her.

'Look where you're going,' a deeply sexy voice said.

And then she felt his hand on her elbow and she wanted to turn and collapse with relief into his arms.

But that would be pathetic—and, more than that, she didn't know who or what they were any more.

'Sev!' She snapped on a smile. 'I didn't know you were back,' she said. 'Susie mentioned it—we just had lunch.'

'What are you up to?' he asked.

'I need to get some rosin…pay my violin rent…'

'Will it take long?'

'No.'

'I'll come with you.'

She really wanted the calm and dark of Signor's to help her collect her thoughts.

'This is my favourite place in the world,' she told Sev.

She smiled, and pushed open the door, hit by the gorgeous scents of wood and varnish.

'Juliet?' a voice called. 'I'll be with you soon.'

'Is it a shop?' asked Sev.

'A workshop, really. He's a luthier. He does all the repairs and makes instruments too.'

Sevandro had never even glanced in the window, but now he was here he looked at this rather odd place that seemed to belong in another century.

He looked at the sign above the counter.

A table, a chair, a bowl of fruit and a violin; what else does a man need to be happy?

Albert Einstein

'I'd need a bit more than that,' he quipped, for Juliet's ears, but a very old man came out and shot him a look, then smiled for the lovely Juliet.

They spoke for ever about her exams, and how well the ensemble were doing.

'We even took a booking for Christmas,' she told him.

And then he asked her about the opera she was rehearsing for.

She had a life here, thought Sev. A good one. And on this day especially he simply could not envisage ever having his own here.

His head was pounding, the scent of varnish too much, and after all that he had found out yesterday, and Dante's reaction today, he had bile churning in his stomach.

Sev glanced at his watch. His flight left soon…

Juliet could almost feel his impatience, and even Signor noted it for he gave her a glance. But finally her rent was paid and they were heading back to the house.

Juliet wondered if he'd even have dropped in had they not crossed paths.

'You'll see a lot of changes,' she said as they arrived at the gates. 'The garden's—'

'I haven't got time for a tour,' he told her. 'I have to fly at five.'

'You should have said. I could have gone to Signor's another time.'

'I don't expect you to drop everything just because I show up.'

'So what exactly *do* you expect, Sev?' Juliet asked, surprising herself with her own boldness.

But his sudden appearance was unsettling. Her exams were done, her life was moving in the right direction, and she did not want an uncertain relationship destabilising that. If she was even allowed to call it a relationship.

'I get that we've made no real commitment...but to not even tell me you're back in the country...'

She looked at him, wanting to be able to say just how much she'd missed him, wanting to do all the normal things a lover might do—only his sudden appearance and his lack of communication with her only proved how far apart they were. Clearly she didn't factor into his days in the way he did hers.

'Imagine if you bumped into me in Dubai and I hadn't so much as told you I was there.'

'I'd be delighted.'

'Really?' she retorted disbelievingly.

'Juliet, you had your final exam yesterday. I didn't want to interfere with that.'

'I didn't realise you were so thoughtful.'

He gave a black smile. 'I assume that's you being sarcastic?'

'Yes,' she admitted, then closed her eyes, hating this row, trying to push aside her insecurities.

She opened her eyes and met his, almost scared by the relief she felt to be held in his gaze, and she registered properly, right then, how much she'd missed him. Every single day. The only reprieve had been when she was lost in her music.

'Look, it's good that you're here,' she told him.

'For eight more minutes.'

'It won't take long. I was going to call… I've got something to ask you. It's a bit awkward.'

'I don't *do* awkward,' he said.

'You'll just have to say if it's an issue.'

She knew he most certainly would.

'Of course.'

'Gio has asked us to play at the memorial.'

'What?' His voice was like the crack of a whip.

'I think it's going to be a bit of an event…'

'What the hell's Gio doing?' His jaw gritted. 'I don't even know if I'll be there.'

'So I heard.'

'What do you want, Juliet?' He came over to her, his eyes more black than silver. 'Should Helene send you my itinerary? Do I have to relay to you some half-conversation I've had with my brother?'

Sevandro halted. His anger was not aimed at Juliet. He had known it would be foolish to come here, and the reason for his visit was not one he'd intended to share with her—at least not face to face.

Yet here they were.

'Look, take the booking,' he said, trying to keep his voice even. 'It's no problem for me.'

He paused, about to say he'd always hoped she'd be there, but it sounded too much.

'I assumed you'd be there anyway,' he said. 'You've been at every recent family event, after all.'

'Assumed?'

He watched her eyes narrow at his choice of word, felt her anger as she approached, and he liked the way she contained herself, how her lips pressed together, how she did not evade the issues.

God, he admired that a lot.

'The last time I performed for your family,' she said tartly, 'we weren't sleeping together.'

And when he should do the sensible thing—tell her why he was here, and about all the hell of the past two days—instead he caved, reverted to ways of old. Because it was so much easier to reach for her, to hold her hips and bring her closer.

'How about now?' he said.

There was no question as to what he was suggesting.

She could feel that he was angry and turned on as he kissed her, but so too was she.

This deep, hard kiss, thorough and intense, with his hands pulling her in, his energy drawing her into his vortex, was a kiss such as she'd never known.

His jaw was rough on her skin and his hands were between them, undoing the belt of her dress, lifting the skirt. She felt a lick of excitement, as if the craving of recent weeks was about to be banished.

But as abruptly as it had started he halted things, pressed their foreheads together, his breathing ragged.

'I ought to go.'

* * *

He must go.

There was no way he could stay.

He'd done far too much of using sex as a quick anaesthetic, and he'd sworn to do better by her.

'I really do have to go.'

'Do you?'

'I don't think me dropping in for angry sex is a good idea,' he said.

'Angry?'

'Yes. Not with you,' he added. 'But there's no tenderness in me today, and I think you'd regret it.'

'Maybe...'

She nodded, suddenly confused. Because she wanted him so badly and somehow he was taking care of her. Because, yes, she might well have regretted it about ten minutes from now, when he walked out through the door. But still there was this strain and desire and ache between them...this longing, still there.

'I don't know,' she admitted.

'I'm trying to be better.'

'Better?'

She could feel her heart hammering, hear his ragged breath, and she knew she'd just glimpsed the escape of rapid sex. She understood now what he'd been inviting her to partake in that first night.

Sex.

Pure escape.

With Sevandro the thought didn't scare her, and yet he'd closed that door to them—chosen a path he generally ignored.

And then he told her why he was here.

'I had lunch with Ella yesterday.'

'The doctor?'

He nodded. 'After we spoke, I called her.'

They were standing together, but no longer entwined. Her dress slipped back down and the dark passion of before was replaced by the pain of real conversation.

'I told her that I had doubts about Rosa's pregnancy. She seemed reluctant to discuss it…reminded me of her oath… but then she asked how it was affecting me. And the truth is that it *is* affecting me—even more so of late.' He took a breath. 'Do you remember you asked me if I was upset when Rosa lost the baby?'

Juliet barely nodded, but her eyes must have told him that absolutely she did, and also recalled how he'd nodded, but said no more.

Now he did say more.

'I was devastated. The baby was the reason we'd married, and though it sounds a shaky reason, I was determined to make it work. Now, when each anniversary rolls around, I don't know if I'm mourning or…'

She nodded. 'I know the memorial's approaching—'

'I'm talking about the anniversary of Rosa's miscarriage!'

Juliet's breath hitched as he interrupted angrily, though she knew his anger wasn't with her.

'Every year I think of what we might have had, or how old our child would be—and then I remind myself that I don't know if it even existed, if I even have anything to grieve.' His eyes flashed like flint, revealing a glimpse of the turmoil he wrestled with. 'When Rosa died I told myself to leave it…that knowing the truth wouldn't change anything.'

'But it does?' she offered.

'Ella seemed to understand why I needed to know and said that she would give it some thought. She called me back and said she would talk to me next time I was home. I explained I was up to my neck in work, and asked could we do it over the phone, but she wanted to speak face to face. There was really no way I could get out of work, without letting a lot of people down, but neither could I wait until the memorial.'

'I get that...'

'So Helene shuffled things about and I flew back. I got in at eleven yesterday and met Ella for lunch. She said she'd looked through Rosa's records but there was nothing she could tell me.'

'I'm sorry.'

'No,' he said. 'Maybe you had to be there to get what she meant.'

His face was pale, and she watched his throat as he swallowed, then looked back into his silver-grey eyes.

'There was no confidence to break because there were no records of any pregnancy or miscarriage. Rosa didn't see any doctor at the practice in the whole year before she died.'

'Sev...' Her mind darted for another explanation. 'Could she have seen a different doctor?'

'No.' He shook his head. 'I was told Dr Romero had taken care of her. I was in Dubai when she lost the baby, so her mother took her to hospital. She told me Dr Romero had said she should rest at their home, so they could take care of her. Lies...all lies.'

'I'm so sorry. Are you...?' What could she say? 'Are you okay?'

'I've been better. I was supposed to fly back yesterday,

but I knew I needed to speak to Dante, and I needed a bit of space before that. So I had Helene move things around again and went to the hotel. Believe me, I wouldn't have been great company last night.'

'I don't need you to be great company…'

She halted, her thoughts all tumbled. She didn't think now was the time to reveal that she just needed his company. Just that. Wanted him good or bad. She pushed those thoughts aside and tried to focus on all he'd told her.

'You didn't have to be on your own.'

He gave her a look that said he didn't quite believe that.

'How did it go with Dante?' she asked.

'I don't know. He was quiet…'

'Perhaps it just needs to sink in.'

'Or perhaps there's nothing left to say. I think we're as close as we're ever going to be. There's too much water under the bridge for us to go back to how we were.'

'Could you stay a bit longer?'

She wasn't asking for herself—well, maybe a bit—but she hated it that he was glancing at his watch when there was still so much here for him to sort out.

'Just a couple of days? It might give Dante a chance to get his head around it.'

'I can't.' Perhaps he saw the flash of doubt in her eyes. 'It was hard enough to get these two days off.'

'Can't you tell Sheikh Mahir…?'

'It's not about Mahir—or Adal.' He looked at her. 'I work fourteen or sixteen-hour days. It's how my life is. And I don't get to jump off the hamster wheel without letting an awful lot of people down. It's like you,' he said, 'in exam mode.'

'That was temporary, though.'

Oh, there would always be practice, and her life would always be busy, but she couldn't imagine living at his permanent frenetic pace.

'I come up for air now and then.'

'I can't for a couple of weeks—but I will be back for the memorial.' He gave her a lighter kiss, a goodbye kiss. 'I wish I'd come here last night.'

Juliet was silent. She wished he'd been here too. Not just for sex but to be with each other, to be there for each other.

'You could come to Dubai,' he said. 'For a few days…'

He was so nonchalant about it—clearly thought nothing of flying her around the world.

'What? You'll pop me on your private jet?' She tried to keep her voice light.

'God, no—ghastly things. Mahir has one. I refuse to use it.' He smiled, 'You'd have to slum it in first class.'

'But will you be able to take any days off?'

'Probably not,' he admitted. 'But we could work something out.' He headed for the door. 'Think about it.'

She could not stop thinking about it.

He'd left her with a glimmer of hope.

He was all she thought about.

Even her music offered no escape.

Then again, Mozart's *Apollo et Hyacinthus* was so emotional—about youth, death, jealousy and betrayal—that instead of crying she just poured all her feelings into rehearsal…

CHAPTER EIGHT

HIS CALLS WERE RARE, but they still made it a gold star day, and her reliance on them still troubled her.

'How are the rehearsals going?' he asked one evening.

'Intense.'

She lay there on the crimson bed. In a couple of days he should be here—though according to Susie it was doubtful he'd even come.

According to her heart, he had to.

But then he'd be gone again.

'Am I interrupting?'

'No...'

She yearned for these moments.

They never referred to his brief trip to Lucca, but she wished he would. They were simply polite and a little formal.

Maybe there had been other women for him?

Perhaps that was why he had stopped kissing her when he had, and all these anguished thoughts were pointless ones. He'd return and not lay a finger on her—as agreed.

'How's work?' she asked. 'I looked at the photos.'

He'd sent her images of a scaled-down version of the new structure and it made her stresses about rehearsals seem small.

'It's incredible,' she told him. 'Well, it will be...'

'We're in the final stages of pre-construction,' he said.

She made herself ask. 'You *are* coming to the memorial?'

'Yes. Dante called and told me that Rosa's family are all going to be there, so he probably thinks I won't show, given what I've told him. He said that Gio would never have invited them if he knew.'

'Will you tell him?'

'Maybe someday, but not now. I'm sure you don't want to see the De Santises and the Casadios all kicking off at the cathedral...'

'No...' He always made her smile.

'Gio wants speeches—I've told him no. You were right. You don't need to hear me giving a speech about how I miss Rosa.'

'I don't care what you say.' Juliet sat up. 'And I do get how tricky it is. Please don't worry about me.'

'I've told Gio no speeches, but I'll do a reading at the cathedral.'

'I won't be at the cathedral. I'm staying back and setting up the instruments at the house. I think everyone else is going, though.'

'It's going to be big,' he agreed. 'I just want it over and done with. I'll come from the airport that morning and head straight for the cathedral. Then I'll stay for an hour or so at the drinks.'

'What if your flight's delayed?'

'Fantastic! Then I'll skip all that and spend the little time I have in Lucca sorting out your "first time" list. I still haven't wined and dined you, after all.'

'We had dinner in Forte dei Marmi and we danced.'

She smiled as they returned to personal conversation…as he soothed her fears. It would seem they were still on. And she didn't care right now if it was just for one more night.

'Oh, no,' he said. 'You're going to be fully wined and dined.'

'Good! But can I change my list?'

'Of course.'

'I don't want a picnic.'

'Believe me, you don't have to worry about that happening. I don't want one either.'

'I thought maybe…'

'What?'

'You haven't called much.'

'I'm trying to let you focus on your rehearsals. I know how important the opera is, and I don't want to land all my stuff on you.'

'There hasn't been someone else for you?'

'Why would you think that?'

'Because you came back and we didn't… I know you were doing the right thing—I mean, not just dropping in for sex, or whatever…'

'It wasn't just me doing the right thing.'

'No?'

'I didn't have any protection with me.'

'If you'd told me that then you'd have discovered that I've gone on the Pill.'

'Damn,' he cursed. And then he laughed. A low laugh, so seductive it was as if his breath was on her ear. 'I wish you were here…'

'I do too.' She was on fire just hearing his voice.

'Do you?'

'Oh, yes…' She tried to rein herself in. 'But it's impossible. I know that…' She let out a sliver of her heart. 'I can't wait to see you.'

'And you shall—in about thirty-six hours.'

'Yes.'

'And we can do all the things we haven't yet done. And perhaps we can talk. You know…ask each other questions we don't have to answer, but can if we want to.'

She took a shaky breath. Was she about to be told it was all too much effort for too little reward? Or…?

'I hope you get some decent practice in,' he said now.

'I will.'

'And I shouldn't say this, but I'm glad you'll be there. Even if it's going to be a hellish day, I'm pleased you'll be there.'

Was she just a diversion?

Something to look forward to for getting through the memorial?

It didn't feel that way.

She wandered around the house, knowing she wouldn't be there soon, loving every wall.

She thought of all the time he'd given her, even while they were apart.

This summer, even when she was without him, she had felt as if he'd been right by her side.

She'd hoped perhaps he'd change his flight and arrive in Lucca the night before the memorial.

He didn't.

Walking along the walls, listening to the church bells calling the congregation to the service, she heard a text land on her phone. It told her he was on his way to the cathedral.

She didn't know whether to send him a thumbs-up or a heart. So she sent both, watching the little pink heart zip off to his inbox while trying hard to hold on to her own.

Letting herself in at the staff entrance at Gio and Mimi's, she smiled as Cuoco came out of the kitchen in his chef's whites.

'You're not going to the service?' she asked.

'I am,' he said, seeming a little flustered as he looked around the kitchen, which had dishes laid out and covered, and notes hanging and timers ticking. 'Me and my team are all coming back straight after communion, but Gio wants us all to be there until then. There may be a little bit of chaos when the guests arrive, but I think we're ready to go.'

'Can I help?'

'No.' He shook his head. 'Don't touch anything.'

'I shan't!'

'*You* get to just sit and play,' he grumbled, being cheeky about her easy job today.

But then he took the cover from one of the beautiful plates and held it out to her.

'*Ricciarelli!*' She groaned when she saw the little Tuscan almond biscuits, so delicate and pretty. 'You're forgiven,' she said, sinking her teeth into one. The orangey tang as it melted on her tongue was sublime. 'I promise I'll only touch these,' Juliet said.

'You seem much happier,' he said.

'Yes…'

And it wasn't just because she would see Sev today. It was as if the pause he'd allowed them had meant she could catch up. Even if they said goodbye tomorrow, it had still been wonderful. That looked-after or looked-out-for feeling had stayed with her since Susie and Dante's wedding day.

It felt a little odd to be alone as she set up the instruments, though it had happened a few times, and it felt very odd to be alone in the home Sev had grown up in.

After collecting some of their equipment from the under-stairs cupboard, she walked through to the dining room and out to the portico.

It was too hot to be playing outside, really, and she wasn't thinking of her fair skin, but more of the instruments. She'd brought her old faithful violin, rather than the beautiful one, as had the others.

She carried things through, bit by bit, trying not to look at the floral displays and memorial portraits. But every time she passed it felt as if eyes were upon her.

She was being ridiculous. And almost to prove it, Juliet turned around to be met by the eyes of Rosa.

And, yes, it would take a better woman than her not to be curious, so she walked over and really *looked* at the other woman.

Oh, she had been gorgeous, with black eyes and beautiful black hair, and she was smiling, so happy and alive. Juliet understood that Sev couldn't be cross with her, that he still wanted to protect her even in death, because it was so cruel that she was gone.

Had she loved him so much that she'd been willing to lie?

It stung to look at Rosa, so she moved on to the portrait of Sev's parents. His father had been as dark-haired as his sons, and she thought he was wearing the cufflinks Dante had worn on his wedding day. Their mother had been blonde, her smile subtle, almost curious, and Juliet thought of her blowing kisses to her son in his school play, embarrassing him a little.

It was a fond thought. It made her eyes fill. And then

Juliet heard the hitch of her breath—for it suddenly felt as if she knew…

Knew what?

That you love him.

No. Juliet shook her head as if to clear it, tried to deny what was being said in her head and in her rapidly beating heart. *I don't.*

Then she looked at Rosa, whose smile seemed a little mocking now.

Of course you do.

And then it was as if the golden feeling he triggered inside her had received its hallmark and was stamped right there, under the dark eyes of Rosa.

She loved Sevandro Casadio.

Juliet walked briskly from the dining room, her eyes a little misty, her face one burning blush, scared to fully admit, even to herself, how deep her feelings ran.

Her hands were shaking as she turned the key to the storeroom and stepped into the dark space. She leant against the wall, as if escaping the scrutiny of his parents' and Rosa's gaze, wanting to hide in there for ever.

She'd thought playing here today would be okay…that she could hold on to her feelings until he'd gone.

She was so wrapped up in her own realisation that she didn't even hear the front door, only footsteps, and she panicked that guests were already starting to arrive when she hadn't even set up.

Then she heard a male voice.

'Go and lie down.'

It was Dante.

Susie's voice when it came sounded strained and teary. 'I can't just disappear…'

'Go and have a rest in my old room. They won't be back for a while yet. Gio's going to be busy greeting people… you can have an hour. I'll be up soon. I'll arrange a drink… maybe something light to eat…'

She heard Susie's footsteps on the stairs, clipping above her, and then Dante calling for a maid.

'They're all at the service,' Susie called back.

It was a little awkward. Juliet would have stepped out straight away, except she could feel her damp cheeks. Of course she'd escaped to the cupboard to cry, to weep alone.

She wiped her tears, and was about to locate the light, when she heard Susie's footsteps as she came back down the stairs.

'Dante, maybe try to talk to him?'

'Susie, let's not do this today.'

'Then when? The baby's due in six weeks.'

'And your blood pressure is high. The doctor said to keep things calm. Go and lie down.'

Juliet screwed her eyes closed, wishing to God she'd stepped out sooner as this rather private discussion took place.

If it had been just about work, then overhearing things wouldn't have mattered.

It wasn't about work, though.

And it mattered very much.

'You can't clear the air unless you tell him.'

Susie was teary again. Juliet put her hands over her ears, because she didn't want to hear this.

'It was *once*!' Susie snapped. 'You slept with her once, and it was long before they were a couple. Rosa tried to trap you too—'

Her voice halted abruptly as the bell at the main entrance rang.

Never, ever, wish to be a fly on the wall.

Juliet stood in the darkness, her heart hammering. Not in fear of being caught, but in dread at what she'd heard.

Oh, she'd known on the day of the wedding that Susie had been holding back, but she truly hadn't wanted or needed to know—still didn't.

Only now she did.

Dante had slept with Rosa. And from the sound of it she'd told *him* she was pregnant too.

She'd stumbled into a secret—just as she had when she'd found out about her father—and she wanted never to have found out. To reach into her mind, into all her senses, and somehow erase what she had heard.

But it was indelibly there.

People were arriving. She could hear Cuoco shouting orders and the waiters getting busy. Almost on autopilot she found the light and dragged Louanna's cello out of the storeroom.

No one noticed when she emerged. If they did, no doubt they assumed that she had arrived with the catering staff.

'They'll be about fifteen minutes,' Dante informed her, coming over to help.

She tried to act as she would have done if she hadn't been here all along...ask the right questions. 'How was the service?' she asked.

'It was...' Dante thought for a moment. 'Tough.'

'Where's Susie?' Juliet asked—as if she didn't know. 'Still at the cathedral?'

'She's having a rest.'

Louanna and the others soon arrived, and as the catering staff took care of the last details the groundsmen opened the gates on the walls as they did their final tune-up.

Before the guests had even arrived, they commenced their playing. And Gio's choice to have the ensemble in the grounds was right for the ambience, if not the instruments, for as they walked along the walls it was as if the music invited the guests in.

The music was ambient, apart from a couple of more sombre selections, and when she saw Sev arrive her heart soared. She fought not to put her instrument down and go over, but then her heart plummeted when she recalled what she now knew. Instead of smiling to him or attempting to meet his eyes she focused on the score ahead and the sounds the group made rather than look up. But of course she could not entirely look away. He was shaking people's hands, thanking them for being there, and then he was standing with a tearful couple, and something told her they were Rosa's parents.

He was doing this for Gio.

And for his late wife.

Sevandro was the strongest person she knew.

She looked at both brothers, standing talking, and knew that if Dante told him it would surely finish them…

So it was time to forget what she'd overheard.

They commenced Pachelbel's *Canon*. Louanna played the same sombre notes on her cello over and over as the other strings played their own separate parts. Yet it was the cello that made the piece so achingly beautiful.

Dante and Rosa had once slept together.

Like the notes Louanna played, the words repeated in Juliet's head, over and over.

It didn't shock her—but knowing the secret scared her. She was terrified of blurting it out in the same way she had with her mother.

Yet how did she keep it?

How did she lie in bed with someone she loved while holding on to a secret?

Two secrets...

After all, he didn't know the depth of her feelings...

Sev could see that Juliet was struggling—so too was he. He would far prefer her to be by his side today. He was exhausted from playing the grieving widower, yet of course he would never bring a casual date to such an occasion.

They needed to work out what they were.

He didn't want to add pressure. He was more than aware that she was staying in his house, and he did not want the home advantage.

Nor to mess up her rehearsals.

He did not quite know what to offer or to say.

He just knew that it could not continue like this.

Susie followed his gaze. 'The music's lovely...'

'Yes.'

Sev took a breath. The sun felt too bright, but he offered a small smile for his grandfather, who had made his way over.

'It is all beautiful, yes?'

No.

'Sevandro, Rosa's parents are here. You have to make a speech.'

'I told you no speeches, Gio.'

But Gio was very old school. 'Do the right thing.'

* * *

Gio made his own speech, talking about his son and his beautiful wife and their gorgeous daughter-in-law. Then he called for Sevandro…

Juliet glanced over, saw the set of his features and knew he'd been landed with this. And she really didn't want to hear it, or make it worse.

'Louanna, I need to…'

'Go.' She nodded. 'There are headache tablets in my bag…'

They worked together a lot, knew when the other was off kilter and covered for each other—and anyway it was just the speeches…

Bloody speeches.

She was angry as she punched out two headache tablets and gulped water. Everything was spoiled. She didn't know how to get through tonight.

But as she went to go back she saw Sevandro going into a room. The same one he had that first night.

She stood there, thinking how she'd wanted to go after him that first day. The pull towards him had existed even then.

Don't tell him…

She said it over and over as she crossed the entrance hall.

Don't tell him…

She repeated it in her head as she pushed open the door.

'Sevandro!'

'Come here.'

His kiss was dark and passionate. His scent was familiar and the effect instant. She was undoing him even as he peeled down her knickers, and she hadn't known anything could be this desperate or instant.

His back was to the door and he was almost kneeling, but he was still too tall so he lifted her instead.

This wasn't how it was supposed to be. Tonight she was meant to be wined, dined and romanced. But the power of him stoked her own, and she wouldn't change a thing.

'Never again,' he said, his voice hoarse with suppressed anger. 'I'm out of here.'

She could feel his fingers digging into the flesh on her hips and knew she was moaning. She was grateful when his hand came to her mouth and she could sob into his palm as she came, and the groan he gave as he released himself into her shattered her again.

They were in a library, she realised as she looked over his shoulder. And although she should be blushing as he let her down, tumbled and shaken by the strength of their unleashed desire, she felt calmer...

'Okay?' he checked, and she nodded.

'Yes.'

'I didn't say much.'

'I don't need to know much.'

She didn't. And he didn't need to know what she'd over-heard earlier.

They didn't kiss, or say how nice it was to see each other again, or that they were looking forward to tonight.

That was separate from this.

'I ought to get back,' she said.

CHAPTER NINE

IT WAS DUSKY as she walked to the house.

The night she had longed for was finally here.

Her and Sev. Together and alone.

No flights to catch—at least until the morning—and no place they needed to be.

Now she walked along the gorgeous familiar streets towards the house she adored and the man she wanted to be with.

She'd felt a little emboldened after their encounter in the library, as if it had proved she could get through and not tell him.

But that had been a temporary escape, Juliet knew…

Tonight was about discovery…finding out more about what the other wanted, what was at the forefront of their minds.

She didn't know how she'd meet his eyes. In fact she felt sick to her stomach as she climbed the stone steps.

She was utterly relieved when he opened the door and she stepped inside, and he took her straight in his arms so she could bury her head in his chest.

'I know it was hellish,' he said. 'I should have thought…'

'It was fine…' She took a breath of him. 'Interesting at times.'

'Very,' he said. 'But it's the last one. I've told Gio no more. Forget about them all now…'

How could she?

They were his family, and she knew more than he.

But she pulled herself back and smiled when she saw he'd changed.

'You're all dressed up,' she said, glad to have something to focus on other than the secret she held. She ran her hand along the sleeve of his immaculate suit, a lighter grey than the one he'd worn for the memorial. 'Are we going out?'

'You'll see,' he said. 'Go and get ready.'

'Sev!' She laughed. 'I assumed we'd stay in. I haven't even thought about what to wear.'

'Your bath is ready.'

'Have you had a maid come in?' she teased walking up the spiral stairs. 'Should I expect petals floating on the surface?'

Oh, there was more than that. There were candles lit all around, and fragrant bubbly water, and a glass of Casadio wine.

It was all so perfect.

If only she hadn't heard what she had.

Juliet trailed her hand through the water. 'It looks gorgeous…'

'Enjoy,' Sev said. 'Are you okay?'

'Perfect.'

'Do we need to discuss what happened earlier today?'

'No.'

She was fine with what had happened in the library— had loved it, in fact. It had been far easier than being here, not knowing what to say.

She looked up and smiled, and thought she'd never

given him a false smile before. She hoped the candlelight masked it.

'How long have I got?'

'As long as you need.'

'I need a hint before I get ready,' she said. 'Where are we going?'

'Somewhere we can talk.'

Damn.

'You're sure you're okay?'

'Of course.'

She stripped off and sat on the edge of the bath in a panic. Somehow she had to hold back from this man who drew her in closer than she'd been to any other.

She felt twelve years old again, with her mother asking why she was in such a mood. Only this was worse—far worse. She was twenty-five years old, and even if Sev might not want her love it was there, and she knew a secret that could destroy his fledgling relationship with his brother.

Spiona.

Tattletale.

That dawn he had called her that it had helped, and they'd laughed, and he'd been able to tease. But she just couldn't see them getting to do that over this.

What should she do?

Learn your lesson. Leave well alone.

Yes, she decided.

So Juliet climbed into the bath and lay there, and it was so perfect she felt some of the tension seep out of her.

Looking around, she saw the twinkling candles and had a sip of wine.

Why would she let something that had happened years ago spoil their night? It was between the two brothers.

Stay out of it, Juliet.

Yes.

She could do this.

Breathing deeply, she closed her eyes, and then she breathed in again and pulled up from the bath and wrapped herself in a towel.

'That was quick,' he said as she came into the crimson bedroom.

'It was gorgeous.' She smiled, feeling a little more like her old self and confident with her choice. She frowned at a large white box on the bed. 'What's that?'

'A gift. I was going to lay it on the bed.'

'What is it?' she asked.

But almost the second she opened it Juliet knew. Soft, silky black velvet spilled out of layers of white tissue paper.

'This is…' She couldn't believe it. 'I thought you didn't buy your dates gifts?'

She was laughing, overwhelmed as she took the beautiful dress out of the box.

'Any alterations it needs can be done. It might be a little big.'

She hung it on the huge antique wardrobe and then found her lacy underwear—the only sexy ones she had. He took them, and she held on to his shoulder as he pulled delicate lace over her still damp skin.

'They're setting up for us downstairs,' he told her as she put her arms through the bra straps and he did up the hooks. He ran a hand down her spine, then turned her around and stroked one aching nipple with the back of his index finger. 'Do you want to do make-up?'

'No.'

'Not those red lips you wore that night?'

She went to the dressing table and put up her hair, and then she painted on those too-dark red lips. She didn't have to hide her eyes—this was just about them.

The dress was perfect.

It went on over her head, and she slid her arms in as he pulled the skirt down.

Then he led her to one of the many large mirrors.

'I love it.'

The scoop neck was higher than on the cream version she'd tried on, and this time her arms lifted easily. There were no pointy bits on the shoulders—he'd got every detail right.

'Oh, I can't believe you did this.' She smiled at him.

'You're going to play beautifully in it.'

'I hope so.'

They went down to dinner. Given the lack of furniture, she wondered where they would eat, but they went out into the late summer night in the cut back garden, with the fountain flowing, stars popping out.

'They want to see you in that dress too,' he said.

And so they sat, a little formal and awkward with the waiters there, but it was so nice to sit opposite him. To talk with him face to face about little things, nice things.

'Thank you,' he said at last, as the lightest lemon tart was served. 'We'll be fine now.'

Finally they were alone.

'How are the rehearsals?' he asked.

'They're going really well.'

'And the ensemble?'

She nodded. 'I think I might be able to call myself a professional musician for real soon.' She took a breath. 'I don't know how I'd have got there without this place.'

'You'd have got there.' He took her hand. 'You are going to be incredible,' he told her. 'I'm just sorry that I can't be there—and not only because I don't do double dates with my brother.'

'Perish the thought...'

She gave a little shiver and the real world impinged, just in a quick flash, with all the problems that awaited.

'Why don't you come to Dubai for a few days?' he asked her. 'We can talk about things there. I'll be working, but it will be easier than here.'

She asked the question she was dreading his answer to. 'You're really never coming back, are you?'

'I don't know,' he told her. 'I think things are better than they have been. The memorial went as well as it could have.'

And perhaps it was a culmination of the events of the day, or just a glimpse of what lay ahead, but her eyes filled with tears.

He took her hand. 'Stop,' he said.

And, yes, they did need to talk, she thought. But it had been such a wrenching day—surely they deserved to simply enjoy this beautiful night and each other.

'We haven't danced yet,' he said.

He opened an app on his phone and music filtered through the garden.

He stood and held out his hand. 'Please?'

Back in his arms, she was in bliss. She would always be happy there.

'It's nice music...' he said.

'Yes...' Juliet wound her arms around his neck. 'I used to play that piece.' Then she stilled and listened. 'Is that me?'

'Gorgeous, isn't it?' he told her.

'You've got my demo tape.'

'I've had it for quite some time.'

And now she was shaking inside as they danced, his hand on her back, her head on his chest, and he told her he found her music relaxing.

'I like watching you play,' he told her. 'I like listening too.'

He kissed her then, on the garden dance floor, until even the private garden would not do. Their lips were waxy with lipstick, and she loved his mouth dark and reddened.

Together they took the spiral staircase and then went into the crimson room, where they closed the door even though there was no one around.

'I've missed you,' she said, and they kissed, soft and slow.

'Undress me, then,' he told her.

And, while she wanted their clothes to somehow melt away, and to be naked beneath the covers, there was a different bliss to be had in this.

She wasn't sure she could stand still and steady if he was undressing her. Just stand the way he did as she removed his jacket and went to place the garment over an occasional chair.

He took it from her and dropped it to the floor.

Juliet was nervous—not because of him, more because she didn't quite understand what was required here.

'Your tie is…'

He smiled as she struggled with the knot, and she wished he'd kiss her, or that she could kiss the olive skin of his neck, but instead she went to deal with the buttons of his shirt.

'Cuffs first.'

'I don't know how cufflinks work.'

'That's fine,' he said, in a way that told her they had all the time in the world.

Only she could feel the energy in the air…could see his erection straining the fabric of his trousers as she dealt with the silver cufflinks. Even his hands were stunning—long-fingered, with neat nails.

'What about your watch? Should I take it off?'

'Please.'

How could removing a watch be a turn-on? How could exposing the veins of his inner wrist make her own skin thrum with desire and her mouth want to lower and kiss his pulse?

Now on to his shirt, and that button by his throat. A very sexy throat. She would have liked to tell him, but pressed her lips closed.

He made her feel light-headed as the fabric parted to reveal the dark mat of his chest hair and her impatient hands tugged the fabric up.

'Perhaps undo my belt?' he suggested.

'You're not being much help.'

'Very well,' he said, and kicked off his shoes and removed his socks. Then he stood still. 'Take your time.'

She was one burning blush as she dealt with his belt and the top of his trousers, trying not to notice the bulge of him. Her nostrils filled with his smoky scent as she undid the last buttons, then peeled off his shirt down long muscled arms.

He took her hand and placed it on his chest, and she felt him warm beneath her palm. She wished her heart was as steady as his. Her eyes were drawn to his flat, dark nipples, and she drew her flattened palm back and stroked one.

* * *

Sev closed his eyes. Her slow perusal was a heady turn-on. And then he felt the wet of her mouth and her tongue tasting his nipple…

And he ached, his restraint becoming unbearable as her mouth moved to his neck.

'Juliet!'

She undid him and pushed down the dark trousers, struggled with the silk boxers and then freed him. She should finish the task, but she was too fascinated, watching as he stepped out of his clothes.

And there was Sevandro, made naked by herself, his narrow hips, strong thighs, black silky hair. She touched the back of her finger to his erection and then ran it along the base, turning her hand and feeling the velvety skin with loose fingers.

'Lift your arms,' he instructed.

'I don't want to,' she said, but she did so.

With practised ease he divested her of her dress, then he unhooked her bra with those skilled fingers. She felt the drop of her bust as he slid the straps down, and in a second she'd stepped out of her knickers.

'Nothing to stop us now,' he said.

And as they hit the bed there was so much lust in the eyes that searched her skin, although his touch was gentle on her breasts.

She didn't have to avoid his gaze any longer. His focus was intently on her, but in a pleasurable way, and there was nowhere to hide in his bed.

He kissed her so softly that it teased, and made her ache for more as his naked body weighted her down from the hips. But from the waist up there was still soft distance. He was up on one forearm and his mouth was tender, his hand stroking her face. There was no trace of the dark passion that had joined them this afternoon…his kiss was sublime.

'I've been waiting for this night,' he told her. 'Waiting for this,' he said, as he slid in unsheathed.

There was a catch in her breath as he filled her…a moan from him as he slid into her tight, oiled space, stretching her. And still he hovered above her as they joined intimately below, watching her.

'I've missed you,' she admitted, saying what she hadn't been able to the last time they'd made love.

'I know.'

He lowered his head and she heard his sigh of satisfaction as he moved within her, as if savouring the sensation, and she savoured it too—the feel of him deep inside her, moving within her, her body curling and arching, her legs wrapping around his.

'I really…' She wanted to say again that she'd missed him, but that didn't quite fit. Why did she cry when he was inside her? Why as he moved faster did she feel as if he were shaking out her secrets? 'I really missed you.'

'I'm here,' he told her, and he shifted, angling himself and delivering a pleasure so deep it made her cry out, had her saying his name.

'Sev…' She was a little frantic, the short word not enough. 'Sevandro…'

She could feel herself tighten, her neck arching back under the deep kiss of him on her throat, and now he was moving faster within her, each thrust a warning, urging her to complete.

'Juliet…' he warned her, and the growl of his tone told her he was close.

She pressed her lips together, unsure of the words she might spill as he swelled within her. As she watched his face contort, heard the groan of his release, she felt a flood of warmth and couldn't hold back. She just gave in to the endless sensations he delivered, her intimate pulses her only response.

He felt every flicker of her orgasm, deepening and prolonging his own, and he pulsed into her, then rested his full weight on the warm, flushed body beneath him.

He lifted his head and they stared at each other.

'I missed you too—a lot,' he told her, still inside her. 'Too many nights.'

She nodded. 'For me too.'

He pulled out and they lay together, and it was the closest he had felt to complete.

'We need to do something about that,' he said, as they lay sated and on the edge of sleep.

'How, though?' she asked.

And there was a tiny note of panic as she tried not to think of the oceans between them, or the closer problems they might have to face, not wanting the real world to impinge.

'Shh,' he said, as if was refusing to break their bliss. 'Let me sort it.'

And this was another moment of bliss.

To fall asleep in his arms and simply leave the impossible to him.

CHAPTER TEN

HIS ALARM WAS UNWELCOME. Pulling Juliet up from where she lay in his arms in a blissful sleep. Then those arms freed her to turn it off, and she lay in that gorgeous place between being awake and asleep, just enjoying the fact that he was here…

And going back.

'What time do you have to go?' she asked.

'Soon,' he said, and kissed her shoulder.

She lay still as he climbed out of bed. She sank back into sleep as he went to shower, but soon came the realisation that their one perfect night was over.

So perfect, she thought, wishing he didn't have to leave just yet. *Perfect apart from…*

There was a feeling of dread she couldn't place, but then, even before she'd opened her eyes, she remembered what she'd overheard.

Dante and Rosa.

She took a breath, tried to recover in herself the woman who'd been able to shut it all out last night, but it was right there in the forefront of her mind as Sev came back into the bedroom.

'I'll make coffee,' she said.

'No time,' he told her, opening up his case. 'Dante and Susie are coming to your opening night, yes?'

'Yes,' she said.

'Then there are four more performances?'

'Yes.'

She lay on her back, watching as he dressed, trying not to think about yesterday and get back to focusing on now.

'How about, after the performances you come to Dubai for a few days?'

She stared at him. When she wanted to nod and say yes, there was just this missed beat where she wondered how she could hold in the secret for days.

'Yes,' she said, but knew he'd seen her hesitation.

'When?' he asked. 'I'm trying to sort a couple of things out with work…with here.'

He sat on a chair to do up his laces but he looked at her as he did so, his hair blacker than normal from the shower and his eyes not leaving her face.

'When?' he asked again.

'I'll have to check.' She was trying to react normally, but there was nothing normal about the secret she held. 'If we've got any bookings or…'

'Check, then.'

She knew she couldn't lie for 'a few days'—and that would mean telling him what she'd learned. And she didn't know how, or even if she should. She wanted time to think about what to do, and bit on her lip as she picked up her phone.

'I thought you were just joking when you asked me before.'

'No.' He shook his head. 'I am deadly serious. Juliet, I'm

trying to carve some time out for us. I get that you're build-ing your career and that your life is here—but mine isn't.'

His eyes never left her face and she felt as if there was nowhere to hide. 'I can't see myself coming back here—not for months—so I'm asking if you want to come to Dubai for a few days. If we can't even manage that…'

There was no way forward for them.

She got that.

But they were so in tune and so honest with each other that of course he knew when she was not.

'Juliet, what's going on?'

She felt like an archer, scrambling for arrows to keep him back—a defeated archer, because she had no arrows and no response except a pale, 'Nothing…'

'Nothing?' he checked. 'Or is it that you would prefer not to answer? Because from the start we gave each other that option.'

They had, and she nodded.

'What does that mean?' he snapped, annoyed now and clearly not wanting to play any games. 'Can you look at me?'

She tried to, but his grey eyes were like a stormy sky, and she could see he was holding anger—who could blame him for that?

'Is there nothing wrong, or is it that you'd prefer not to answer? Which one is it.'

'I'd prefer not to answer.'

'Fair enough.' He pulled on his jacket. 'I'd better go.'

And he really didn't play games. Because there was no shared little kiss to pretend things were fine—he just took up his suitcase and wheeled it to the door.

She sat with the crimson sheet around her, recalling her decision never to tell him.

But then the thought that had helped her last night appeared again. Something that had happened so long ago shouldn't be ruining things now—and yet it was.

'Sev…'

His hand was on the door handle, and he paused.

'What?' His shoulders were tense, jaw gritted, but he half turned.

'There is something wrong, but I don't know how to tell you.'

'You just say it.' He turned around. 'What's going on?'

'I found out something,' she said. 'I overheard it…it's about you.'

Sort of. But it was going to devastate him, she knew.

'Am I supposed to be sleeping with Ella, just because we went out to lunch?' He shook his head. 'I know how people talk.'

'It's nothing like that.'

'Juliet?'

'Not so much about you…but about Dante and Rosa.'

'For God's sake!' He let out a half-laugh. 'It's just gossip.'

She shook her head, and something must have told him this might be real, because she watched the colour leach from his face.

'Something happened between them before the two of you were married. Long before.'

'Juliet, Dante has never dated anyone from Lucca. I told you…'

Then he swallowed—the same way he had when he'd told her there had been no baby.

'Who told you this?'

'No one told me. I overheard it. Dante thought Rosa was trying to trap you because the same thing had happened with him.'

'When did you hear this?' he asked. 'Who...?'

'Please don't ask. I wasn't meant to hear it; I wish I never had. I'm only telling you this because—' She stopped.

'Because...?' he persisted.

But he didn't need her declaring her love even as she hammered him with this news. And so, she bypassed the real reason and gave him the one that loving him would lead to.

'I think it's better that you hear it from me. If he ever tells you...'

'Why would he tell me?' he barked. 'If it's been more than a decade since he and Rosa...?' He briefly halted, but there was so much fury the unsaid word still hung there. 'Why would he bother to bring it up now?'

'I shouldn't have said anything...' She gulped. 'I've made it worse.'

'Worse?' He shook his head. 'You've made it easier for me to leave.' He flicked his hand, perhaps in the direction of the family home, or maybe Dante's. *'Bastard.'*

'Sevandro!' She jumped out of the bed as he reached for his case. 'Don't rush off.'

'I've got a plane to catch.' He shrugged her off. 'And now I can stop being guilted into doing the right thing by my family and by Rosa's family. I'm done. I'm out of here. For good this time.' He glanced over his shoulder. 'I might see you in Dubai if you can spare a couple of days.'

Juliet was too upset to cry—if it was possible to be such a thing.

She just sat in the crimson bed, holding her knees and

waiting for the sky to fall. The genie was out—and, worse, she was the one who had let it out.

She thought of her parents—the fights, the rows—and of changing schools, losing her home, losing friends.

She cast her eyes around the crimson room, then climbed from the bed, peering out of the window as if expecting to see a convoy of flashing lights and emergency vehicles on the ancient streets. But there was gorgeous Lucca, bathed in a golden light, the tower and its holm oaks standing steady, oblivious of the changes surely to come.

Surely?

Yes. Everything she loved was about to be taken away.

Again.

'Corso Garibaldi...' Sev said to his driver.

A loaded catapult, he asked to be taken to Dante's address. He knew damn well where Juliet would have heard the secret. No doubt Dante had told Susie, and Susie...

Susie.

Pregnant and asleep, she would not need him pounding at the door...

'Ferma la macchina,' he ordered the car to halt.

The driver stopped the car and the world that had been spinning since Juliet had told him came back into focus—only with the twenty-twenty vision of hindsight.

Dante had been trying to talk to him. Not just on the eve of his and Rosa's wedding but in the weeks before...

As bloody as their fight had been, he'd always thought they ought to have been able to move past it...as brothers should.

'I'll be back in a bit,' Sevandro said, and got out of the vehicle.

He really was out of here, he decided. After today he would never be back. And so now he walked along the walls for one last time, and looked out to the mountains that had taken his parents and wife, and loathed the scoffing noise he made when he thought of Rosa.

But it was too hard to go there, so he loathed instead his smart Alec comment about seeing Juliet in Dubai if she could spare him a few days…

And then he gave up thinking and sat on a bench and stared out at the verdant hills that looked so peaceful but had taken so much.

Perhaps it was better to leave without a fight, so to speak.

He would never be back here—in that moment he was sure.

And so there were things to be taken care of before he left.

His flight would be taking off minus one first class passenger, he thought, when he left the little store in the centre of Lucca, having taken care of Juliet in the best way he could think of in such a raw state.

He was about to call Helene to arrange a new flight when he saw a flash of purple and stopped outside a florist's, looking at the citrus colours and blushing pinks.

There was no scoffing noise now when he thought of his late wife.

No more putting off what he had for more than a decade.

He'd never known what to say.

And as he stood at her grave he still wasn't sure.

Rosa De Santis

'You wanted to keep your family name,' he said aloud, placing down the flowers.

In Italy some women kept their own name, some took their husband's. It hadn't troubled him either way back then.

Now it did. Now that the red mist of anger was fading, he could see the influence her parents had had on her, and knew that Rosa would never have come up with that plan alone.

He spent some time there at the grave, his bile when he thought of his late wife gone. Seeing things so much more clearly now.

'What do you want me to do?' he asked, but of course was met with silence.

He thought of Rosa's fears, how she'd cared so much what others would think.

'Don't worry...'

He made her a promise he would keep. It was the best he could do for her.

'Dei morti parla bene...'

Of the dead, speak well.

He always had.

'I shall continue to do so.' This would stay with him. 'Rest now,' he said.

Peace made—at least with Rosa—he flew away from the hell and chaos of home,

And yet there wasn't the usual relief he felt when leaving.

Flying above the clouds, he kept going over and over things—not the past, and not Dante, not even his time with Rosa, or any of that.

Her words.

Juliet's.

'I'm only telling you this because...'

Was it love?

And if it was love, then where did they start?

Even in Dubai he worked ridiculous hours—had commitments from early morning till late at night. If the contracts all went ahead every minute of his next two years would be accounted for. How could he even consider plucking her from her blossoming career to a lonely ex-pat life there?

He couldn't.

He wouldn't do that to her.

He thought back to last night, their bodies still locked together, the closest he'd felt with another person, their souls searching for answers, for more time together and less lonely nights, and recalled the slight panic in her voice when she'd asked, *'How, though?'*

'Signor Casadio?'

He turned at the flight attendant's voice, realised they had landed without him even noticing.

'We're disembarking.'

Usually he was the first off the plane.

Today he would be almost the last.

Because Sevandro sat there on the Tarmac in Dubai, not sure where home was.

Letting himself into his apartment, he opened up the safe and took out the little stone Dante had given him. He held it up to the light, thought of his brother as a little boy in the jeweller's, always in trouble, always the charmer, always led by emotion.

He took out his phone.

'Dante.'

'Hey,' Dante said. 'You're back in Dubai?'

'I am.'

Sevandro waited for his brother to mention the memorial

yesterday, or the conversation they'd had the other week when he'd told Dante he'd been right.

He was met with silence.

Now he understood why Dante found it so difficult to talk.

'How's Susie?' he asked.

'She's okay,' Dante replied.

And Sevandro found that he frowned, because he did still know his brother—at least a bit—and there was something not right with his tone.

'Just a few weeks to go, yes?' he said.

'Yes.'

'Is everything okay?'

'Of course.'

'Because you know you can…'

He paused. Of course Dante would not be able to tell him anything, or confide any fears about his wife. The secret his brother had kept had forced a wedge between them, and Sevandro could see things more clearly now.

Thank God he hadn't gone around there with all guns blazing. Instead, from the safety of Dubai, he offered better words.

'I'm always here if you need to talk.'

'I know.'

But instead they had a bland conversation, just as they had for the last decade—he asked about Gio, and the winery, and Dante asked him how the house sale was coming along.

'I saw the gardens have been done—it looks incredible.'

'I'm not so sure,' Sev admitted.

He didn't like how it felt now that the light shone in. He'd liked the dark space where he and Juliet had…

'Are you going to have it styled?' Dante asked.

'Probably.'

They spoke for a few more moments.

Just the same conversation they'd been having for a decade. Perhaps it was a bit easier than it had been, but really they still spoke as if they were strangers on a bench in a park.

Now he knew why.

Then he called Juliet.

'I'm sorry,' she said immediately. 'I shouldn't have said anything.'

'Stop,' he told her. 'You have nothing to be sorry for.'

'I am sorry, though. I called Louanna and there's a spare room in the apartment. The guys are going to help me move my things today.'

'Why would you do that?'

'Because we both agreed that my staying here was only meant to be until after my exams, and because I know that you're going to resent me for telling you what I heard.'

'Resent you?' he checked. 'I don't do that.'

'Maybe not, but it will change things.'

'What things?'

'Everything.'

'Change can be good,' he pointed out.

She gave a small disbelieving snort. 'I hate change! Anyway, I've got performances next week to prepare for. I can rehearse with Louanna.'

Sevandro thought what best to say. He did not want to add pressure, and the half-baked plans he had in his head would help no one.

He needed to think things through properly.

'Nothing has to change for now. You're not to let anything mess up this week,' he told her. 'Go and practise…go to your rehearsals. You certainly don't have to move out.'

'I think I do.'

'Is that what you want?'

'Yes. It is. Are you at work?'

'No. I'll go in tomorrow. I'm just thinking a few things through.'

'Did you say anything to Dante?'

'I just spoke to him,' Sevandro said.

Hearing her tense breath, he knew his decision to call Dante first had been the right one. At least he could put her at ease there.

'We didn't talk about anything much.'

'Will you ever talk to him about it?'

He evoked their agreement. 'I'd prefer not to answer that one.'

'Fair enough.'

'But I can say for certain that I won't be doing anything before the operas, so don't worry about seeing them at the weekend.'

'Okay…'

She didn't sound sure.

'Sevandro, I didn't tell you just to unburden myself.'

'I know that.'

'I wanted you to hear it from me. If Dante does ever talk to you—'

'He won't.' Sevandro shook his head. 'I'm pretty certain we're past all that. Can I ask you something?' he said, and heard her inhale. 'Actually, two things.'

'Sure.'

'When I asked about you coming to visit me here you were hesitant. Is it because you don't want to prolong things between us?' He walked through to the bedroom and saw the coffee silk sheets had been replaced by russet-coloured ones...the colour of her most intimate hair that only he had explored. 'Or was it because of what you'd found out?'

There was a long pause. 'The latter.'

'That's good to know.'

He could invite her to come now, tell her the offer was still there. But suggesting a few days in Dubai to celebrate the end of her exams and opera performances sounded not enough—it sounded vague, and not like any plan he would make.

And as for a lifetime here...

He looked at the gap in the skyline, knew full well the commitment it would take to fill it. He'd been heavily debating the same with Sheikh Mahir in recent weeks.

'What was the other thing?' she asked.

'Do you know how brave you are? After all you went through with your family, it must have been awful to overhear what you did. I am sorry you had to find out and be the one to tell me.'

'No, no,' she said. 'That's just it. I *wanted* it to be me.'

He didn't quite understand why she said that, but now Juliet had a question for him.

'Rosa...' He heard the tension in her voice. 'I feel as if I've made your memories of her worse...'

'It's okay,' he said, touched that in the midst of this she would think of a woman she'd never met. 'I've been thinking of Rosa too.'

He closed his eyes, stunned that he could share such a deep thought with her—that on this too bright day, when colours were too vivid and the world too sharp, he could somehow confide in her.

'I didn't go straight to the airport; I sat on the walls for a couple of hours. I realised it was Rosa's family. They always wanted the land…the wineries merged. There are feuds that go way back.' He could see it so clearly now. 'After the accident, when the wills were read, I remember how furious they were when they found out that my father hadn't owned a single vine. The winery was always in Gio's name. Even after her death they were thinking of how they could benefit from her.'

'Poor Rosa,' said Juliet, and then went quiet. 'Do you think she was worried you'd find out there never was a baby?'

'I was already finding out,' he said, and he held that unexamined heart that this morning had felt as if were being stabbed under a gentler inspection now. 'I would have got her away from them… I think she knew that.'

'You'd have been fine with a loveless marriage?'

'I would have been back then. I told you—I'm a selfish bastard.'

'You're not.' Then she asked him the same question he'd asked of himself. 'What if you'd found out she'd slept with Dante?'

'We'd have divorced, but I still would have got her away from her family. Well, that's what I told her this morning. I went to the cemetery and took flowers. I said what I did on the day I put her in the ground—that she can rest. And I think she can now.'

'That's nice.'

'Now, I've got a lot of work to do,' he told her. 'So, if I'm quiet for a while that's why. For now, stop worrying about my family—and good luck with the move and the operas.'

'Thank you.'

'Do *not* break a leg...'

She managed a shaky laugh.

'Juliet, it's going to be okay.'

It could never be okay...

He hadn't said when they'd see each other again, and nor had he repeated his invitation to her to spend those few days with him in Dubai.

She had an awful feeling she'd been let down gently.

That Sevandro had said goodbye.

On the evening before her big performance she sat with Susie at a pavement café, sipping Limoncello spritz as Susie topped up her sparkling water.

'How is it being back at Louanna's?' Susie asked.

'It's working out well, I think.' Juliet nodded. 'We're rehearsing a lot.' It helped take her mind off things...though not quite. 'I need it. I just can't...'

'Can't what?'

'I feel a bit wooden,' Juliet admitted. 'Technically, I'm playing okay. And while it's good to have Louanna pushing me, I do miss Sev's place...' She shrugged, refusing to think about the gorgeous home and its owner. 'I liked practising there. I could get into my music more.'

'Well, I doubt you could now.' Susie tore apart her *panettone*. 'Sev's getting it styled.'

'Oh?'

She picked out an ice cube from her glass and sucked on it, trying not to react, trying not to think of the gorgeous house with strangers coming in, and trying not to ask questions about Dante and Sevandro.

'He's not coming back,' Susie said.

Her ice cube crunched as she bit it, and she saw Susie's blue eyes sparkling with unshed tears.

'Apparently he took flowers to Rosa's grave…and what with his speech at the memorial…'

'I didn't hear it,' Juliet said, oh-so-nonchalantly, her face burning as she thought of them in the library. And then, breaking her own rules, she pushed for a little more information. 'What did he say?'

'Just how much his parents had enjoyed life… Rosa too. How she'd been on her way to Fashion Week…how they all knew that *la vita è bella*. Life is beautiful.' Susie sighed. 'Who says that at a memorial service?'

'Life *is* beautiful, though,' Juliet said, and couldn't help but smile, pleased that Sevandro had said that. She was proud that he'd stood up and respectfully said he would not play the game any longer.

'I was hoping that things might be sorted between Sev and Dante for the baby arriving. The wedding went so well. But really…' Susie took a breath. 'It's not all Sev. Dante shuts down too.'

'It's between them.'

'Yes.' Susie nodded. 'They were so close, though, and they both lost so much.' She picked up a serviette and blew her nose. 'Gosh, I'm teary.'

She looked tired, Juliet thought, and she felt worried. It wasn't her sixth sense kicking in, as it had when she'd first thought Susie was pregnant—she'd overheard her and Dante, after all, and knew her blood pressure was high.

She tried to ask in a roundabout way, but she wasn't very good at delving, and as they said goodbye Susie still hadn't told her of any concerns.

'We'll see you tomorrow night,' Susie said as they

hugged each other goodbye. 'You're going to be fabulous; I know it.'

Oh, Juliet wasn't so sure...

It wasn't the best pre-opening night. She tried to sleep, but kept checking her phone, wishing her parents would message and wish her luck.

Not really.

She was lying to herself.

She kept checking her phone in the hope that Sevandro would call and she was trying to resist calling him, aching to hear his deep voice, feel the sense of calm he brought whenever he was near.

'You look dreadful,' Louanna informed her when she came into the kitchen the next morning.

'Thanks! I'm going to get some coffee...buy some more rosin.' She rolled her eyes. 'We've certainly been going through it.'

Louanna had been pushing her to practise, which was good, but at times she could see the little frown lines on Louanna's face as she played. Could feel her worried glances.

Juliet wasn't playing well.

She was holding back, scared to put her heart into it for fear she'd completely break down.

She walked into the little shop that was her favourite place in the world. Well, it used to be. The crimson bed was now her favourite—but she was trying not to think of all that.

'Signor!' Juliet called. *'Sono io, Juliet...'*

'I won't be long,' Signor said from the workroom, and Juliet told him there was no rush.

It was lovely and dark, and so peaceful in here, and she wandered around, looking at the beautiful instruments.

'Are you ready for tonight?' he asked as he came out.

'I hope so.'

'Nervous?'

'A bit,' she nodded. 'Maybe not enough?'

'It's a beautiful piece, though rather dark at times.'

'Yes,' she said—because 'dark' was how she felt when she practised and she was scared to go there, to let loose her already off-kilter emotions and really pour herself into the piece. 'I'll get there. I just need some more rosin—and also to pay my rent.'

'No.' Signor frowned. 'That is your violin now.'

'It's not. I know my rent's due next week.'

'But it isn't,' he said.

And then the world seemed to stop when she was told her friend had paid her account in full.

'My friend?'

She thought of Susie, who kept trying to press gifts on her. But no, Susie wouldn't even know where this place was. Surely it wasn't…?

'He doesn't agree with my sign.' Signor laughed. 'We agreed to disagree.'

She glanced at the familiar Einstein quote and recalled what he'd said. No, that would never be enough for him.

'Sevandro was here?'

'Si.'

He went to fetch a leather folder and took out a ledger. Juliet stared at the figures and then saw his black spiky signature.

Yes, Sevandro had paid her account.

Yes, the violin was beautiful, and everything she had once wished for.

But really she was simply relieved to have an excuse to call him. She stepped out into the sun, almost folding in relief at the sound of his voice.

'Juliet?'

'It's too much,' she said. 'I just went to pay my violin rent and...'

'You weren't supposed to find out until next week!' He laughed. 'I hope I haven't messed up your pre-performance calm.'

'I'm not calm.' She took a breath. 'Maybe I am. I don't know... But I can't accept this.'

'Then donate it to a charity shop,' he teased. 'Or post it to me here. Of course you can accept it. How are the rehearsals going?'

'Not great,' she admitted. 'I feel...'

'What?'

'Like a fraud.'

'Fake it, then.' He laughed again, and so did she. 'You can do it.'

'I'm not so sure.'

'I know you can.'

For a sliver of time she felt their closeness again, felt warmed by his voice, felt emboldened and back on their beautiful Mars—but then he told her he had to go.

'I have to go into a meeting now. Don't break a leg.'

'Sevandro, wait,' she said. 'I can't take it.'

'It's already yours,' he said. 'It always was.'

He closed his eyes as his private phone rang again, telling himself to stay back...to give her the space she needed.

Certainly she did not need to know what he was dealing with here.

Helene came in. *They're waiting*, she mouthed, and he nodded, about to turn off his phone. But then Dante's name flashed on the screen...

Given the nature of his meeting, he had every reason to let it go to voicemail, and yet for whatever reason he quickly took the call.

'Dante, hey. I can't—'

'Sev.'

Brothers know.

Not everything—not every detail of each other's lives—but brothers who were close knew, and the husk in Dante's voice was reminiscent of a day long ago, and immediately Sevandro knew something was very wrong.

'It's okay,' Sev said to his brother, shaking his head at Sheikh Mahir, who had come into his office, and turning his back. 'What's going on?'

'Susie went into labour last night. They've tried to slow things down, but they think the baby will be born soon.'

'What else have they said?' he asked, and then listened as his brother brought him up to speed.

'Are her family coming?'

'They don't know. I'm going to call them later. Susie is quite upset, but she doesn't want anyone to know yet. I'll tell Gio and Mimi when we know more.'

It dawned on Sev that his brother had called only him.

An older brother was still required at times.

'She's going to be fine,' he responded with certainty. 'Both of them are.'

'You don't know that!'

Sev heard the sneer...knew Dante was scared.

'I believe that—as must you when you're with Susie.'

'Yes.' Dante took a steadying breath.

'Don't let her see you're worried.'

'Okay.'

'Juliet doesn't know?' he asked.

'Juliet?' Dante's voice was bewildered. 'I've just told you we haven't…' Dante paused, obviously remembering they had the opera tonight. 'We're supposed to be going to her opening night.'

'Maybe let her know you won't be there?'

'She won't even notice—it's a sell-out.'

Sev closed his eyes. Of course Juliet would notice. He thought of her looking up to the empty box and finding nobody there for her. Though of course Dante had far more on his mind right now and wasn't really thinking about cancelled plans.

'Sev?' Dante's voice broke into his thoughts. 'The other week, when you told me that Rosa had never been pregnant…'

'Don't worry about that now.'

'Let me speak,' Dante said. 'I need to say this. I'm going to be a father soon and I want…'

Sev closed his eyes and thought back to her words.

'I'm only telling you this because…'

Thank you, Juliet.

Now he understood why she'd said what she had about wanting to be the one who told him. So he'd be prepared for a moment such as this. So he'd know what to say when his brother finally reached out to him.

Dante cleared his throat, clearly determined to do this. 'I didn't know how to react. Or what to say. I've wanted to talk to you, but I've been worried about Susie. She thinks I should tell—'

'Dante,' Sev cut in. 'It's okay.'

'It's not, though…'

'But it is,' Sev said.

'No, there's something I need to tell you.'

'I already know.'

'You don't…'

It was a conversation that brothers never wanted to have, but the distance and the silence between them was killing them.

'Dante, I know about you and Rosa.' There was silence. 'I *know*.'

'How?'

'Doesn't matter.'

'How long have you known?'

'That doesn't matter either. It's time to move on. You're going to be a father soon. I'm going to be an uncle. Things are very different now. Go and be with Susie. If it helps, tell her that we're fine. Call if you need me, or call Helene to get hold of me.'

He could hear the shake in his brother's breathing, the same sound he'd heard in it at their parents' funeral, and Sev said now what he hadn't been able to then.

'*Ti sono vicino.*'

It meant, *I'm close to you*, or *I'm right here.*

And if he was going to be there for his brother, then Dante needed to be there for him too.

'Before you go back to Susie can you do one thing for me?'

'What?'

Sev looked at the time. Even if he left now there wasn't

a hope of him getting to the concert, but he couldn't bear the thought of Juliet looking up to see an empty space.

She needed to prepare for that in private…

'Can you let Juliet know you won't make it tonight?'

'Sure.'

'She'll understand, but…'

'I'll call her now.'

'Thanks,' Sev said. 'Then get back to Susie.'

He sat for a moment, then buzzed Helene.

'Sheikh Mahir is getting impatient,' she told him.

'Could you ask him…?' He stopped, and thought of the board sitting there, waiting. He knew Mahir would not appreciate being asked to come to Sev's office. 'Could you arrange a private room, and advise the Sheikh I need to speak with him?'

Things were not going to plan.

Or rather things were happening rather ahead of schedule.

He'd wanted her performances to be over…for his work situation to be in better order…for him and Dante to…

That last one was already taken care of.

He opened the privacy drawer on his desk, and seeing the little gift he'd had made didn't jolt him, or look like a foreign object. He picked it up and saw the diamonds glinting and the one tiny ruby.

The perfect plan would have to wait.

Juliet needed him now.

It was time to deal with the *other* because…

He was certain.

Juliet had told him because she loved him.

CHAPTER ELEVEN

FLOWERS WERE BAD luck before a performance.

But Sev knew she wasn't superstitious, and so all through the morning and into the afternoon she desperately hoped for some.

She ached for more than his call this morning. She wanted Sev's reassurance…for him to tell her she'd got this.

She'd laid out her dress, and was checking she had everything she needed for tonight, when her phone rang.

It was, though, the wrong Casadio…

'Of course I understand.' Juliet was touched that Dante had thought to call her when he was so worried for Susie and the baby. 'Please give her my love.'

Yes, she was touched, and worried—she felt all of those things—but she felt so lonely as she sat on the bed in her old apartment.

She opened her bedside drawer, where she'd put her copy of the ledger, just to see his signature. That little piece of him…

But now, she read it properly—not the monetary sum… she dared to look at the date.

He'd paid this the morning he'd left.

And, thanks to Signor's meticulous record-keeping, even the time was noted.

He must have gone there before he got the flowers for Rosa's grave, or maybe the other way round...

It didn't really matter who'd come first.

He'd been saying goodbye to Rosa.

And there was but one other realisation she could come to—at nine twenty-seven that same morning he'd been saying goodbye to her.

The floodgates opened then—horrible tears that she'd held back not just since he'd left, but since the morning of the service, when she'd realised fully that she was in love with him.

Maybe she wasn't meant for love, Juliet thought, frantic with tears. Possibly it would have been better never to have met him than to be so raw and tender now, with her soul in agony.

She was gulping, crying more than she had at the age of twelve—because this hurt more than it had when she was little.

Really, she'd been alone since then.

And she'd got through it.

She was still here. Even if there was no one to see her... even if he was gone.

She was here.

She could do this alone—just as she always had.

And she was not quite alone.

She thought of Susie and Dante, who had such a wonderful reason not to be there tonight, and then ran a hand over the gorgeous violin that Sev had bought for her. It had felt like too much at the time, yet it felt like a comfort now.

Their time together had been wonderful, and beautiful, and everything she had ever wanted.

She would play tonight.

Enjoy tonight.

Pour all her troubles into her beautiful violin.

There was a knock on her door and Louanna came in with a glass of water. 'I'm heading off. See you there?'

'Yes.'

'You're okay?'

'I am now.'

Right now she had the biggest performance of her life—and, yes, the show must go on.

She slid on her new underwear.

It was gorgeous, but a little more *her*—silky, but plain, with not a bow or a shred of lace.

Then she did a light make-up—mostly to cover her complexion, which was a little blotchy from crying. Almost as a warning to herself that her crying jag had to be over, she put a little mascara on, and some lipstick, and then pinned her hair back from her face, but left it loose down her back.

The dress was heavenly, and as she looked in the mirror Juliet felt like a real musician.

'Come on,' she said to her gorgeous violin—the one Sev had bought for her, though she decided not to think about that right now...not with mascara on. 'You too,' she said, and took her spare and most trusty back-up. 'Just in case.'

Lucca was so beautiful as she walked to the *concerto* hall. It was the only place she knew where it was normal to walk in a velvet gown, carrying your instruments, and people smiled and wished her good luck with no real idea who she was. It was enough that she was on her way to make music in a town where it was revered.

* * *

Backstage was tiny and crowded—and the most exciting place on the planet.

This planet.

Mars was possibly her favourite other planet—but she wasn't allowing her head to go there tonight.

And then it was time for the orchestra to file out, and she took her place. She could see the hall filling up, glanced up and saw the empty box, but then quickly looked away.

Soon the buzz of the audience was drowned out by the wonderful sound of an orchestra tuning up.

She was here. She had made it. Even if there was no one to see her.

Then the conductor entered to applause, and the orchestra were invited to stand and take their own applause. It was a gorgeous tradition—to look out to the people you would play for, to invite them to share in this night.

She tried not to look up again to where Susie and Dante would have been, but foolishly she did—and then she saw him. Yes, it was dark, and, yes, he looked a lot like his brother... But she would know him anywhere.

It was impossible. She'd spoken to him just a few hours ago. And, having tracked his plane that dreadful morning, she was quite an expert in flying times from Dubai.

But he was here.

Somehow.

And even if she couldn't see him properly, she knew he was looking straight at her.

And then his head moved in that small nod of encouragement, and she wished to God she hadn't worn mascara.

Or perhaps it was a blessing that she had, because it

forced her to blink and snap out of the gentle spell he'd placed her under and take her seat.

Juliet was magnificent.

She didn't look up at him once.

He could see her head moving as she gave in to the music, and while he didn't like opera—or rather he didn't *love* it—tonight he decided he did.

Of course he'd never tell Mimi. She'd sing him to death.

At the interval a fruit platter and some herbal tea were placed by a table at his side. Given this should have been Susie's seat, Sev realised he was being served her order. Thankfully Dante had ordered whisky and dark chocolate.

The second act commenced, and even while eating chocolate-dipped strawberries he conceded that he might come to agree with the old luthier's sign. Einstein, with a few modifications, might just be right. A velvet chair, and chocolate-dipped fruit, and a violin—so long as it was being played by Juliet.

He could watch her every night for the rest of his life.

In fact, he very much hoped that he would...

Be calm, Juliet told herself as she headed for the stage door. *He's here because of Dante.*

Probably he felt sorry for her.

But she was delighted, and she couldn't hide it when she stepped out. 'You! I never imagined...'

'You were incredible,' He told her. 'I can't believe I might have missed it. What an opening night!'

One kiss, she told herself as he pulled her into his arms.

She was weak for his mouth. His kiss was so delicious

she had to stop and put down her violins so she could focus on the sheer pleasure of it.

They were going to sleep together. She knew that as their tongues reunited and his hands roamed the black velvet. There was a desirous energy to their kiss, and his mouth was so insistent. Their necks craned to be closer, nearer. He was stroking one velvety breast…

This kiss was far from a greeting.

But if she slept with him then she'd have to start getting over him again.

'I am not being your Lucca lover,' she said, peeling back. 'Any news?'

'Loads,' he told her. 'Come on.'

They walked down the cobbled lanes, holding a violin case each and holding hands. She was wired, and happy, and simply refusing to let trouble spoil it. She licked her lips and his peppery scent was in her nostrils again.

'Okay…' she conceded as they headed for his house. 'Just tonight.'

'That was easy,' he said, and they both started to laugh.

'How on earth did you get here? You were in Dubai when I called.'

'I spoke to Sheikh Mahir…explained the emergency.'

'Was he okay about it?'

He made a wavering gesture with his hands. 'Not at first… But he's very much a family man, and he gave me a loan of his private jet to get here fast.'

'Ghastly things!' she teased. 'But wonderful when your brother needs you and there's a baby on the way!'

He gave her a very strange look.

'Juliet, I didn't fly back because of the baby.'

'Of course you did!' She laughed. 'You and Dante can both deny it all you like, but you love each other really.'

'I guess... But I'm not overly involved.' He gave a short, incredulous laugh. 'Juliet...'

But they were at the gates to the house—and, no, they were not having this discussion in the street.

'Inside.'

He pushed the door open, and as Juliet walked into the entrance hall she felt her nose twitch with annoyance—because, yes, it had been styled.

It looked fabulous.

Dammit.

So did the lounge. The grey sofa was gone and there were two large navy silk ones, and beautiful rugs like those she might have mentioned. There was even a piano...

'You liked my suggestions, then?'

'I did.'

She almost wished she'd never seen the house come to life like this. Now she'd remember it for ever, stunning and gorgeous and with all the things she loved in it.

'It's perfect.' She gave a slight sniff. 'You didn't waste much time.'

'No. I got Helene on to it the day you moved out.'

'The same day!'

'I was actually relieved that you moved out...'

The chances of her being his Lucca lover tonight were rapidly diminishing, she thought, and she was about to tell him that.

'We have a lot to discuss,' he went on. 'Maybe a few rows. This way you don't get to storm off so easily.'

'Why would I storm off?'

'Hopefully I've negated any need to, because I've been in some serious talks with Mahir,' he told her. 'I knew I couldn't ask you to come and live in Dubai.'

'Live there!' Her mouth gaped. 'Sevandro, I haven't even been.'

'I've been asking you to come.'

'For a few days!'

'To see if you like it. Juliet, I knew I couldn't ask you to give up your career, and I know you love it here...'

She was back in that audio booth again...or maybe it was Mars. Because she could hear his voice, and she was looking into silver-black eyes, but he was telling her about pulling back from billion-dollar contracts. Not pulling out. Just stepping back.

'When did you decide all this?' she asked.

'On the Tarmac in Dubai.'

'And you didn't think to discuss it with me!' Her mouth gaped. 'Aren't we supposed to be able to tell each other anything?'

'We have our little amendment,' he reminded her.

'But I've been missing you. I was on the floor crying over you this afternoon.'

'You still made the performance,' he pointed out. 'I didn't want to mess up your preparations for the *concertos*, nor to discuss things with you till I at least had...'

'A plan?'

'I guess...'

She saw he was being very honest.

'My life was not geared up for two, Juliet,' he said. 'There wasn't anything to discuss until I'd sorted things out. How could I ask you to come to Dubai with the hours I work? And what if you wanted to live here...?'

She swallowed, realising what he meant.

Lucca was her home.

She'd built a life she loved here; her career was just taking off.

'We could have spoken about it,' she said.

'We are going to talk about it,' he affirmed. 'I have no plane to catch, no alarm to set, and I have forty-eight hours.'

At first she laughed, because he spoke as if he had managed to carve out an entire month to focus on them. But then her laughter faded. She knew how big this was for him, and realised how much he respected her career—how he'd worked to bring the very best of himself to the negotiating table.

'So, this plan...' She was shaking a little. 'Sevandro, I would live anywhere with you.'

'I know that,' he said, and then he led her to one of the gorgeous navy couches, where he sat down and then pulled her onto his knee. 'And I knew if I was asking you to do that for me, then I had to be prepared to offer you the same.' He looked right into her eyes. 'I would live anywhere with *you*!'

Her breath hitched. 'Even here?'

'Yes.' He nodded. 'I can say that in all honesty now. Even here. I always chose not to examine my past, but with your help I have now, and I'm okay with things. I can live here—so long as it's with you.'

'You mean it?'

'I more than mean it. This is your home, and I can't wait to share it with you.'

'What about Dante and...?'

'We're fine. I am so grateful to you for telling me. I

know why you did it. Because it was better I heard it from someone who has my heart in mind.'

'And I do.'

'Dante called this morning. He was about to confess, but thanks to you he didn't have to. I told him I already knew.'

He gave her a kiss that told her of his relief and gratitude.

'Thanks to you, I didn't say something I would later regret.'

'That's good.'

'We all know everything now!' he said. 'Thanks to my little *spiona.*'

Sev, or Sevandro, was so many things. He said what no other ever could, and he went to places in her heart no one else could touch, and he turned the impossible into a smile.

'I landed to the news that I'm an uncle. Dante and Susie have a little boy—Eduardo…'

Juliet felt as if she was spinning with happiness, and yet she sat still held in his arms.

'I'm an *uncle.*'

He rolled his eyes, but she knew he was both pleased and proud.

'And Mahir's fine. The agreement I've been trying to broker is that I will hand over more to his son. It was all very tense, but then I told him about you…about the opera opening night, and nobody being there for you. He came with me to the airport and we talked a few things out.' He pulled her to him. 'Juliet, *you* were the emergency he lent me his jet for. Dante and Susie were meant to be there, but when I found out they couldn't…'

'Seeing you up there,' she told him. 'It meant everything. And I didn't even know you loved me then.'

'*I* knew,' he said. 'I was getting things in order, while you did what you needed to.'

'You know I love you.'

'Of course—you were looking at wedding dresses the morning after you lost your virginity.'

'I was not.' She thought back, blushing all over again. 'No, I was not.'

'You soon will be.'

She gave an excited nod, and she thought this must be love because neither had to ask.

It was just happening!

'We'll get a ring later. This is to celebrate your first official first chair performance tonight.'

He took a little black box from his pocket, and she knew she really was being looked after.

The brooch was exquisite—a tiny silver violin, encrusted with diamonds. Her eyes were too blurry at first, but as she lifted it from the box she saw one dark stone... one little ruby for the bridge.

She knew it was from his mother's ring.

'I'll treasure it for ever,' she told him staring deep into his eyes.

'As I shall treasure you.'

He would take the greatest care of her heart.

EPILOGUE

SHE WAS TINY. With little knots of red hair and huge navy eyes that were attempting to focus as she stared up at her father. Her chin trembled, her sweet rosebud mouth quivered, and Juliet looked up to Sev.

'You're okay,' he told their daughter, whose chin stopped wobbling as she got back to attempting to examine his face. 'It's all just a bit new.'

It was a whole new world.

From her hospital bed, Juliet looked out at the stunning skyline. The Dubai sky looked as if it were on fire. The sunset was spectacular, lighting the buildings red, orange and gold. And there was the new father's work in progress—it was going to be stunning.

They'd hoped to have their baby in Lucca—but of course Sevandro had stepped *back*, not *down*, and Juliet loved it here too. He'd been right—there was a wonderful music scene in Dubai, and she was a substitute in an orchestra here as well as at home.

Home was Lucca.

Dante was running the winery now, and still trying to reel his older brother in. Lately he seemed to be succeeding...

'Soon you'll meet the rest of your family,' Sevandro told

his daughter, then tore his eyes from their tiny baby. 'I can tell them to come tomorrow?'

'No need. I can't wait for them all to meet her.'

'Girls are easier,' Sevandro had said, delighted when he'd found out he was having a daughter and was not going to have to worry about all the stuff boys got up to. 'You don't worry about them as much...'

She and Susie had shared a glance, and Dante had rolled his eyes.

'She'll have you wrapped around her little finger,' he'd told his brother.

And now they'd messaged that they'd arrived, and Juliet took her beautiful daughter from her very calm husband.

He'd been incredible through the birth, even when it hadn't quite gone to plan!

Nothing about this journey had fazed him.

Well, if it had, it hadn't showed.

Yet.

'Are we going to tell them her name?' she asked.

'Yes!'

In they came. Susie first, her eyes brimming when she saw the newest Casadio, and Gio all smiles and tears too. Dante was holding Eduardo, who had dark curls and huge brown eyes. He peered at his cousin, then swooped in for a kiss, as almost all two-year-olds would.

'Gently...' Susie said, then swooped in too, and asked for a cuddle. 'Oh, she's perfect... How was it?'

'Worth it,' Juliet said.

'You weren't planning a Caesarean, though?' Susie checked.

'No!'

She was still a bit dazed, but so thrilled to have the people who loved them the most here on this day.

'Are your parents...?' Gio started, but Mimi stopped him.

'Gio, get Eduardo.'

Sevandro did it, picking his nephew up and making a fuss of him as Juliet looked out of the window for a moment, wishing her own family could have been like this.

She looked at the brothers. Dante was asking how it had all gone and Sevandro was nodding, explaining that she'd just needed to be born, and that perhaps she'd been a little flat when she came out, but she was perfect now.

'Good,' Dante said, and came over and looked at his niece. 'You scared your daddy,' he said quietly to the baby.

Brothers *do* know.

'She scared Mummy too,' Juliet admitted, then looked down at the little pink face and the one tiny hand peeking out. She was absolutely worth all the fright in the delivery room.

'Do we have a name?' Susie asked.

Sev looked over to her—just making sure—but they had discussed it at length. Even though Sevandro had frowned when she'd first suggested it.

'We do,' he agreed, taking the baby. 'Mimi,' he said.

Juliet looked at her, smiling in the background, staying well back...

'Sorry?' Mimi said. 'I am listening. I was just looking at her curls...'

'Her name is Mimi,' Sevandro clarified.

'After the opera?' Mimi checked.

'After you.'

They had thought about his mother's name, or his grandmother's, and had gone around in circles with old-fashioned names and more modern ones.

Juliet had kept going back to one, and finally she'd said, 'I know she and Gio have only recently married, but she's been in your lives for a long time…supporting you all, loving Gio.'

'It will go to her head,' Sev had warned with a smile.

'Good.'

And now there was no attempt to stay back. Mimi came over and scooped up her tiny namesake and started to sing to her.

'What have you done?' Dante said to Sev, and they shared a small eye-roll.

They were back to being brothers.

When Juliet got tired, Sev had no compunction in shooing the happy lot out.

'Are you okay?' he asked her.

'A bit tired…but yes.'

He sat on the bed and they had a small kiss, and a very big gaze at little Mimi, who was getting hungry…or needed changing…or whatever it was that made her squeak and wriggle.

'She's so pretty…' Juliet was fascinated, touching her slender fingers. 'I think she's going to play the violin…look at her chin wobbling…'

Sevandro didn't say anything. If he had it might have come out a bit hoarse.

Of course he loved little Mimi, but it was at that moment that she took his heart and melted him, and also terrified him, and all the other things love did.

'God…' He breathed out sharply and put his head right

down next to hers, breathing in her new baby smell. 'Never scare me like that again.'

'Girls are easier, huh?' Juliet checked. 'She's fine.'

'Yes...' He looked up, checked in. 'You?'

She nodded. 'You?'

'Completely.'

* * * * *

Did you fall in love with
Italian's Cinderella Temptation?
Then make sure you check out the first instalment in
the Rival Italian Brothers duet
Italian's Pregnant Mistress

And why not explore these other stories
from Carol Marinelli?

His Innocent for One Spanish Night
Midnight Surrender to the Spaniard
Virgin's Stolen Nights with the Boss
Bride Under Contract
She Will Be Queen

Available now!